O'Rourke's Revenge

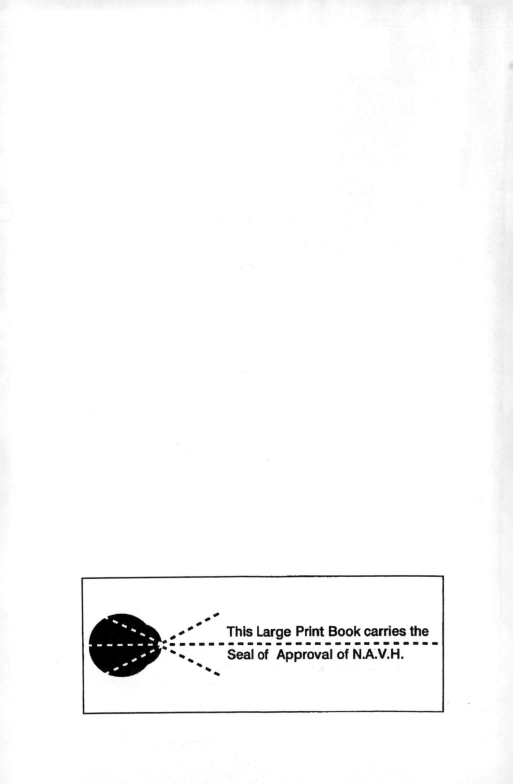

This Large Print Book carries the Seal of Approval of N.A.V.H.

O'Rourke's Revenge

L. J. Martin

Published in 2005 by arrangement with Pinnacle Books, an imprint of Kensington Publishing Corp.

Wheeler Large Print Western.

The text of this Large Print edition is unabridged.
Other aspects of the book may vary from the original edition.

Set in 16 pt. Plantin by Christina S. Huff.

Printed in the United States on permanent paper.

Library of Congress Cataloging-in-Publication Data

Martin, Larry Jay.
    O'Rourke's revenge / by L. J. Martin.
        p.   cm. — (Wheeler Publishing large print westerns)
    ISBN 1-59722-076-0 (lg. print : sc : alk. paper)
    1. Revenge — Fiction.   2. Large type books.   I. Title.
  II. Wheeler large print western series.
  PS3563.A72487O76 2005
  813′.54—dc22   2005016407

O'Rourke's Revenge

As the Founder/CEO of NAVH, the only national health agency solely devoted to those who, although not totally blind, have an eye disease which could lead to serious visual impairment, I am pleased to recognize Thorndike Press* as one of the leading publishers in the large print field.

Founded in 1954 in San Francisco to prepare large print textbooks for partially seeing children, NAVH became the pioneer and standard setting agency in the preparation of large type.

Today, those publishers who meet our standards carry the prestigious "Seal of Approval" indicating high quality large print. We are delighted that Thorndike Press is one of the publishers whose titles meet these standards. We are also pleased to recognize the significant contribution Thorndike Press is making in this important and growing field.

Lorraine H. Marchi, L.H.D.
Founder/CEO
NAVH

* Thorndike Press encompasses the following imprints: Thorndike, Wheeler, Walker and Large Print Press.

One

He stepped up to the heavy iron gate, taking a last breath of stale confined air as the grizzled old man who'd walked him as far as allowed called out, "Don't do it, old pard. You'll die tryin', and they ain't worth spit, much less dyin' over."

"See you in hell, old man," Ryan called, waving over his shoulder.

"Hell? Why, hell's fire, ol' pard, I'm already there."

Ryan O'Rourke shaded dark brown eyes from the burning afternoon sun with a scarred and calloused hand. He scratched a two-inch-long stubble of beard, sure he'd upset a happy home by sending nits scattering with the attack of broken filthy fingernails. Two years ago he would have repelled from a human who smelled as he did at the moment: vinegary, musty, like meat gone bad. But that would soon change, as would his ragged pants and shirt. He'd managed to keep the beard short by sawing it occasionally with the rusty top of a peach tin. In Yuma Prison, knives and razors were as scarce as honest politicians.

Ryan knew a bit about that low-life animal, having served in Prescott as a territorial deputy marshal for three years before he took up his recently vacated career: two years — busting caliche limestone and granite for the first year, then graduating in the second to mortaring the chunks into walls and cells. But that was behind him, literally, as the arched flat-iron-barred gates of Yuma Territorial Prison creaked shut — a gate called the sally port by many — closing him out rather than in.

He stood quiet for a moment, breathing deeply, savoring the air of freedom and the view of Yuma City just below. He consciously tried to exhale the anger that had been seething deep in his gut, but it wouldn't be so easily expelled. He wondered if it ever would.

"Good luck, O'Rourke," Max Snider said.

He'd called out through the grates. Max was a guard, but a fair-minded man — one of a kind in Yuma — who had even the prisoners' respect.

"Thanks, Max."

The burly man, who had fought for the

8

Rebel cause as had Ryan, gave a half-hearted salute, then turned and walked away.

Five in the afternoon and a hundred five in the shade was a hell of a way to be turning a man out into the July desert, but nonetheless Ryan could barely wipe the wry smile off his face, no matter how his stomach bubbled like a cauldron, a brew of boiling hate laced with the spice of unrequited revenge.

As he moved down the hill, each flop of his worn brogans released a puff of flour-fine dust, the bane of his miserable existence for the last two years. God, he wished for clean blue skies, clear water, green grass, and trees.

They matriculated you out at five so they didn't have to feed you the miserable wash that passed for soup at six, and so you'd miss the stage, which left Yuma only once a day, mid-morning — not that most released prisoners had the money to ride the stage — on the slight chance you might have the money and vacate the town before the merchants, of which there were only a half dozen in the rodent-ridden burg, got their pound of flesh from you.

The prison warden had made that pact

with the city fathers so a man would be likely to spend his two dollars in release money in the little pueblo of Yuma, then would have to work for near-nothing until he gained the cost of fleeing to kinder climes. On alternate days the stage was headed east, then west.

The ramshackle shacks and adobes of Yuma City, formerly Arizona City, lay only a hundred yards away on the smoke-tree-lined banks of the muddy Colorado River, the site of the ferry. Across the river and a mile north was Fort Yuma, formerly Camp Independence, and before that Fort Calhoun in honor of the senator John C. The fort only housed a skeleton contingent.

Near the fort lay the ruins of Mission Puerto de la Purisima Concepcion, with ghosts of Franciscan monks from decades past. To the east lay hundreds of miles of harsh desert, two hundred miles of hell to Prescott or Tucson; to the west, just across the river, the scrub-oak-and-chaparral-dotted foothills of the Sierra Madre rose, and 170 miles across them, San Diego overlooked the cool Pacific Ocean.

California, the land of gold and honey. Any prudent man chose the route to Warner's Ranch, then on to San Diego over the one to Gila monsters, Mojave green rattlers, and circling turkey vultures.

But Ryan O'Rourke had seldom been accused of being prudent. Besides, sweet revenge lay east.

One of Ryan's twelve cell mates, Padraig O'Shannasey, a lifer who killed his wife as she was preparing to run off with an officer, had been a grizzled old sergeant who'd served at Fort Yuma when it was active and had fought the Pimas and Maricopas and Apaches. Paddy was the last prisoner Ryan had exchanged words with as he headed for the gate. Ryan had paid close attention to the old pioneer, talking with him for hours on end, even to the point of learning the location of a number of springs and seeps that hadn't made the maps.

It was said that any man who could survive a year in Yuma could do a year in hell and come out spittin'. Ryan had survived two — each day of which he grew harder, tougher, and more resentful, and he was a hard man when he entered. He had been among the third group of prisoners to arrive at the new territorial prison at Yuma, and spent most of his time there building stone walls and additional cells for those who would follow — after a few months of busting rocks, a labor intended to bust his spirit. Twelve men to a seven-by-eighteen-foot cell on hard sawn-timber bunks stacked three high, a flat-iron-barred window on one end and an arched flat-iron-barred door on the other.

A ten-dollar gold piece resided in his brogan under a leather liner, the same place he'd stored it when he'd first passed into the stone and iron cage that had been his castle and keep for those years, and keep was the right word in all its connotations.

In addition, the territory of Arizona bestowed two dollars on every departing inmate, enough to get you far enough into the desert to die, or far enough into the state of California that you'd never want to come back to Arizona, which seemed to be the plan. Either suited the Arizona territorial government just fine — dead or gone was what they expected of you. A dozen men had accommodated the first desire and died in prison during the two years O'Rourke had served — the records said consumption, tuberculosis, debility, tumor, shot while attempting escape, typhoid, or stabbed by a fellow prisoner. None of them said half-starved and half-cooked in the isolation of the infamous "dark cell," a windowless oven; worked to exhaustion; or beaten to death.

Those in power wielded the pen, as it always was and always would be.

Ryan had been carrying over a hundred dollars in gold on him — or rather under the seat of the prison wagon driver, the rolling monkey cage, in a strongbox with other prisoners' valuables — when he arrived at Yuma, but what wasn't stolen by the head bull, Ike McGillicutty, was stolen by other inmates, all except the single gold piece — there were precious few hiding places in a cell with a dozen men. He'd wondered why they'd laughed at him when he asked if the money could be kept in the warden's safe during his internment.

Had he not been good with his hands, having dealt faro for a couple of years before, and some even while serving as territorial deputy marshal in Prescott, he would have lost the ten also. But a little sleight of hand kept it on his person, and out of the greedy gaze and grasp of guards and inmates alike.

But Ryan was smiling for the first time in many months, smiling for three reasons. First, and most importantly, he was free. Second, he could finally get his revenge on the four men who'd wrongly sent him here

— and the one here who'd made him live lower than a snake's belly, the sadistic guard, Iron Ike, who'd made his life a living, breathing hell for the last year. And third, he had plenty enough money for a bath, a shave, a bottle of Who Hit John, and a decent meal.

Ryan had made the mistake of calling the big man Fat Ike instead of Iron Ike, and it had cost him dearly.

Five men, all in the territory of Arizona, then he could head out for Montana, where his aunt's family, the McCabes, had a ranch and job and fresh start awaiting him — and with luck, he'd be taking a woman with him.

After a bath, shave, and beefsteak, he'd figure out what he was going to do, and just how prison bull Iron Ike McGillicutty was going to die.

One thing he knew for sure. The big man wouldn't die easy; he'd die slow, hard, and sorry for his sins against God and, more particularly, against Ryan O'Rourke.

Just outside the sally port stood a guard shack, empty at the moment as neither deliveries nor engraved calling cards were being accepted this late in the day. Forty yards to his right on an elevated mound rested a thirty-by-forty-foot guard tower —

actually a squat building, but it rested atop a stone mound that elevated it above the height of the adobe walls of the main yard. At the apex of its roof was another small lookout, a widow's walk had it been on the East Coast. It enjoyed the best view of any perch on the prison grounds, if looking at the harsh prison grounds and parched hills could be considered any kind of a good view — the Colorado River and its tree-lined banks being the only relief from dust and rocks.

Ryan could see the bulky form of Iron Ike standing there in the shade, glaring at him, his ham-sized fists shoved into his sides. Ryan paused and glared back, then slowly raised his right arm and slapped the crook of it with his left hand, an "up yours" gesture for which he would have spent a week on hard crusts and water in the dark cell had it been done while he was inside.

Ike didn't flinch; he merely glared, until finally he couldn't stand it and yelled out in that deep, gruff voice that Ryan had come to hate.

"Have yer fun, O'Rourke. You'll be back, and I'll have mine."

Ike turned and ambled out of sight.

Ryan adjusted the rope that was his belt,

then spun on his worn heel and headed down the road into town.

He heard Ike's gruff voice ring out behind him. "You'll be back, you Irish trash."

First things first. A bath, a shot of whiskey, and a chunk of beef that he could get his teeth into.

He hadn't walked fifty yards when he eyed a wagon stalled by the side of the dirt track. The wagon and its canvas cover were decorated with painted signs — red, blue, yellow, and white. The largest said TINKER, but under that in smaller letters read SILVERSMITH, MAKER OF FINE KNIVES, DR. LEVY'S WHOLESOME BITTERS, then VIOLIN CONCERTS, and on and on until you'd think it was a wagon train full of craftsmen rather than a single wagon.

A stooped old man rounded the two mules, stopping to take the muzzle of one in his hands and nuzzling it with his gray-bearded face, as another man might his toddler child. The man's beard was a fastidiously trimmed Vandyke, and his mustache was curled and well waxed.

He looked up and nodded at Ryan as he approached, then offered, "Top of the day to you, my friend."

"And to you, sir."

Ryan was determined to get to the store and invest a dime in a cake of soap and a half-dollar in a bottle, then on to the river, and he wasn't thrilled to be slowed in his quest.

"I don't suppose . . . ?" the old man queried.

Ryan sighed, but stopped. "Suppose what?"

"I don't suppose you'd have the time to lend a frail old man a hand?" The old man extended a thin-fingered hand, offering to shake.

He did look a mite frail, but Ryan was determined. He took the hand, surprised at its strength, but shook his head.

"Friend, I haven't had a decent bath nor a beefsteak in two years. Would you deny me . . ."

The old man's smile was ironic, but he was nodding.

"That's plain to any, friend, but I'm a man in need of a hand, and by the looks of yours, they've seen hard work. You might be coming out of that place" — he motioned toward the prison with his head — "but you look to be an honorable sort."

Ryan showed him calloused and cracked palms.

"Hard work? Hard as the hubs of hell,

friend," Ryan said with a slight snarl, but the old man's smile was infectious, and it had been a good long while since Ryan was referred to as an "honorable sort."

"Did you hear the story of the tavern owner?" the old man asked.

"No, sir."

"Well, he served his customer a pint, and the man spit it out. 'That's terrible,' the customer said. 'And to think I paid good money for that slop.' " The old man had a twinkle in his eye. He continued. " 'Well,' the barkeep said, 'you think you got trouble, friend, I've got thirty barrels of the stuff.' "

Ryan laughed.

"So," the old man said, "you think you got trouble?"

"What's your problem?" Ryan finally asked.

"*L'chaim!*" he said enthusiastically. "You'll slip into heaven's back door, no matter your sins."

TWO

But his enthusiasm was short-lived.

The old man sighed deeply, then shrugged.

"*Oy veh.* The hubs of hell have nothing on hard compared to the hubs of this old wagon. I believe this damnable sun and desert have welded my wagon nut on, and I need to pull the wheel to tighten the iron tire, as it's about to end up in the road. It seems Jehovah is testing me once again."

Ryan eyed the old man. "You mean pull it to take it down to the blacksmith?"

"No, sir. I mean to tighten it. I've the makings of a small blacksmith shop right here in this fine well-traveled Studebaker, but I can't do the job of work without the wheel being off."

Ryan shrugged and led the way around the wagon. The old man had the forward gee side ready to jack up, and a wagon wrench in place, but it was only a twelve-inch tool, and would get little leverage on a tight nut.

Ryan plopped down and positioned himself so he could get all his weight into the wrench, put a foot against a wagon spoke, and pulled. He stopped and took a deep breath, then pulled again with all his might. Finally, he stopped and looked up at the old man.

"I declare, that nut's as stubborn as those mules are sure to be."

The old man was leaning down, his hands on his bony knees, his beard hanging to mid-chest.

"Those mules are my family, younger, so please do not flap your tongue at them. They'll get me to San Diego. Are we gonna get her free, or just gab?"

"For a fella doing all the leaning, talking to a fella doing all the work, you'd be a sassy sort."

"Age has its rewards," he said, smiling again.

"How about heating the nut?" Ryan asked. "Have you tried heating it?"

"I have not, but that's fine thinkin'. Sit and rest yourself and I'll fire up my kiln."

Ryan leaned against the wagon wheel as the old man removed a small but obviously heavy kiln from the back of the wagon and set it up behind the drop gate. In moments he was pumping a small bellows. Just as

Ryan was about to doze off, the smell of smoke assailed his nostrils. He opened his eyes to see the old man was holding a lump of glowing charcoal against the nut with a pair of small tongs, blowing on the ember to keep it hot.

Finally he moved back.

"Give her a jerk, friend."

Ryan put his back and shoulders — rock-hard from busting and hoisting rocks — into it, straining until the veins stood out on his neck and his face reddened. The nut suddenly gave, and Ryan almost rolled in a backward somersault. He came up laughing, then self-consciously wiped the smile from his face. It was strange, smiling. He'd had nothing to smile about in a good long time.

"You okay, friend?" the old man asked, his runny eyes twinkling.

"Fine as Sunday morning," Ryan said. This time he smiled freely. "I'm free as that buzzard circling up there, and I'm heading for a bath and beefsteak."

"Go with God," the old man said.

Then he eyed Ryan cannily. "I don't suppose you'd be interested in purchasing a fine bone-handled work knife, a folding knife, or a firearm? Or maybe a two-bit bottle of Levy's Tonic? More good grain alcohol in a pint bottle of Levy's than in a quart of whiskey."

"You got a five-dollar sidearm?"

The old man laughed so hard the ends of his curled mustache quivered.

"I've a fine twelve-dollar Smith & Wesson model with kit, and it's a *metsieh* at that."

"A what?"

"A bargain."

"Maybe, but more than my pocketbook can stand. Can I help you get that tire off?"

"I can handle it from here. I owe you a small favor, young man, and I wish you luck."

"And luck to you, old man. I hope you're in heaven an hour before the devil knows you're due," Ryan said with another laugh.

Ryan would have tipped his hat had he had one, but instead he waved and moved on down the hill, across Yuma's single street to a store with an ANDRE'S MERCANTILE sign, where he used one of his dollars to buy a cake of soap and a bottle of Diamond Back whiskey, getting forty cents change from a handsome young woman. Without bothering to respond to the girl, who tried to sell him a pair of canvas Levi's and shirt for his second

22

dollar, he left and dropped down the slope behind the store into a clump of smoke trees lining the river's edge, sheltering the spot from view of the few buildings.

In moments, he was stripped to his long underwear and waist-deep in the slow-moving brown, cool water.

He spent an hour sipping the bottle in intervals between trying to scrub the stench of the prison out of his hair and off his body. When he finished that, he went to work on his ragged clothes, until he had them back to somewhere near their original drab gray.

He pulled them on wet. Even though the summer sun was touching the top of the Sierra Madres to the west, it was still plenty hot, and he knew he'd be dry before he'd reached Ramon's, the single saloon and restaurant in the town. In moments he was standing before the adobe building that served as a saloon. It had been added onto with a board-and-batt sawn-timber structure, both sides sporting a red-tile roof.

The bottle was half gone when he pushed through the batwing doors of the saloon. He'd been wrong about the heat, as he was still damp with his clothes clinging to him.

He stopped short just inside the doors, relishing the odor of tobacco smoke, letting his eyes adjust. The big broad back of Ike McGillicutty was leaning over the plank bar, two other guards standing beside him: a tall, lanky redheaded man whom Ryan knew only as Mr. Parsons, and a short, solid man built like a hogshead barrel who was named Shott, but called Shoat behind his back by the prisoners. They were the worst of the lot at Yuma.

All of them smoked cigars and sipped foam-topped beers. An eighteen-inch mesquite club with a knot on its end the size of a man's fist hung on a thong from the left side of Ike's belt, and a .44 was strapped to the right. He turned slowly to face Ryan and smiled broadly.

"Howdy, Irish. Now, what was that motion you made at me when you was ushered out the front gate?"

"That motion," Ryan said, "was a wave good-bye . . . and good riddance."

"I'll be wanting to have a word with you after I finish this beer."

"I got nothing to say to you, McGillicutty."

"It's still Mr. McGillicutty to you, Irish. And it always will be. I figured you'd'a limped halfway to San Diego by this time . . . 'cause I hear you're not welcome back in Prescott."

"I'll be on my way soon enough, and the where of it is no business of yours."

McGillicutty pulled the short club free from his belt and shook it at Ryan.

"When I finish my beer, ol' Betsy here and I are gonna come looking for you, O'Rourke."

"I ain't yer whippin' boy no more. You should know that here and now."

"We'll see." The big man turned his back and went back to his conversation with the other two, but he glanced back over his shoulder and eyed Ryan, still standing and glaring at him.

Ryan could smell the odor of beefsteak wafting out of the wide doorway into the connecting restaurant, and as much as he wanted a piece of Ike's hide, he wanted a beefsteak even more — and he'd already tasted that mesquite too many times. As much as his backbone shivered with the itch of retribution, he was unarmed and in Ike's territory, and Ike was bracketed by hard men who worked for him. Ryan had to use his head.

Deciding discretion was the better part of valor, or revenge, Ryan ignored the big man. Instead, he gave them his back, crossed the room, and disappeared into the room next door; a room holding four tables each surrounded by six chairs, and another door leading to an outside kitchen. He could hear Ike's deep guffaw behind him, joined by the other two, but ignored them.

Only one of the tables was occupied, by what appeared to be a miner and his family: a plump rosy-cheeked wife and three cherubic young children.

Ryan took a seat with his back to the wall, placing his half-empty bottle in front of him, and nodded at the young Mexican woman tending the tables as she approached.

"Beefsteak, Señorita, thick and rare, *por favor*. Potatoes, how-some-ever the cook has them, and a fat slice of apple pie as an encore."

"Encore, Señor?"

"After the steak, please. And coffee, hot, thick, and black. And a glass, please. Empty."

"A tin cup is all I have. The pie is from dried apples," she said.

"Apples is apples, and a tin cup will do fine," Ryan replied.

She brought him the cup, just as the miner rose from the table across the room.

Ryan could hear the muffled voice of the woman.

"Don't you dare, Silas." The man crossed the room to stand across the table and stare at Ryan.

Ryan ignored him and half-filled the glass, then let his eyes wander up to meet the man's.

"You'd be wanting something?" he asked.

"You fresh out of that hellhole?"

"I am. My debt, false as it was, is paid in full to the territory of Arizona."

The man smiled. "There ain't never been a guilty man in there, or any other prison."

"Can't speak for the rest of them."

"What was you in for, and how long did you do?"

Ryan eyed him up and down. "You keepin' a journal, starting a newspaper, or just a curious type?"

"Nope, I'm looking to hire a man, and you could be him. You're big enough to eat hay and dump in the road. The question is, 'Are you as willin' as you are big?' "

"Never been much bothered by work. I killed a man in Prescott, in a fair fight, but he was a prominent man and the town and the jury wanted somebody to pay a price."

The man studied him carefully for a moment. "You couldn't have done much time, as the prison's only been accepting guests for three years."

"I did two, although it seemed twenty. I think it was mostly to get me out of town. Like I said, it was a fair fight."

The man stuck out a calloused hand. "I'm Silas Jenkins."

Ryan accepted the hand and shook. "Ryan . . . Ryan O'Rourke."

"The little lady and I got us a lead mine, back in the hills a bit. You looking for work?"

"It's that or walk to Prescott. You offerin' work?"

"Dollar a day and found. And it's the only job I know of hereabout. And like I say, you're big enough." He eyed Ryan, realizing the man had arms the size of powder kegs, wide shoulders, and a narrow waist. He had shaggy black hair and dark, dangerous eyes. But he also had a gentleness, the way he ate and handled himself. Silas had already decided that Ryan was a man who'd give as good as he got, good or bad.

Ryan shook his head.

"Grubbin' in a mine like a gopher for greaser wages? I'm big enough; now the question is, 'Am I dumb enough?' "

"You don't look like no Emperor Franz Joseph nor a university professor, friend. If'n it makes any never-mind, you'll be grubbin' alongside me. I wouldn't ask anything of a man I ain't willin' to do myself."

"Fair enough, Mr. Jenkins. When do I start?"

"I got an ore wagon out front. You can ride in the back with the young'uns and the supplies. I'll advance you enough for a pair of work pants and good brogans afore we head out."

The girl set the steak and potatoes down in front of Ryan, and Jenkins continued. "And I'll pick up the price of that steak. But I warn you, it's rabbit on our table" — he lowered his voice — "and Mrs. Jenkins there ain't much of a cook."

Ryan laughed. "I'd bet she's a mite better than what I've come used to these last two years. I'll be along, soon as I finish this grub. Presuming those three fellas in the saloon leave me be."

"You already courtin' trouble?" The miner's smile faded.

"I'm not courtin' it, but it seems lately to follow me like a bad odor. They're guards from the rock castle, and it seems I rubbed a raw spot on them at one time or another."

"I don't want no trouble."

"You do as you wish, Mr. Jenkins, and I'll do what I have to. And, God willin', I surely won't bring no trouble to you and yours."

The miner shrugged, then returned to his table. Ryan could hear the woman chewing on him like a dog worrying a bone. But he ignored them and got serious with the pound of beefsteak.

The miner and his family got up and left the table and the restaurant, without speaking again — and Ryan presumed his job prospects went with them. Ryan took his time, savoring every bite. He did need the work, but this was the first real meal he'd had in two years.

He finished the last bite of the pie, then looked up to see Ike McGillicutty standing in the doorway separating the restaurant from the saloon, and he was slapping his hand with the hated chunk of polished mesquite and smiling.

Three

McGillicutty's two cronies stood behind him, smiling like they were entering a high-class French brothel.

Ryan stood and stretched. "That's a fine meal," he said to no one in particular.

"You paid yer bill yet, Irish?" McGillicutty asked.

"Damned if there ain't a lot of curious types hereabout," Ryan said.

The Mexican girl hurried over from the door to the kitchen, holding out her hand. Ryan placed the second release dollar in her palm.

"That's a half-dollar for the steak, pie, and coffee, and a dime for you, lass. You'll be owing me a quarter, dime, and nickel."

She nodded, flashed him a quick but worried smile, and hurried out the door. In a moment she returned and handed Ryan his change. He pocketed the dime and nickel, but held on to the quarter.

"This would be what . . ." McGillicutty said, "two . . . or three dozen times . . . I've had to take Miss Betsy here to teach you some manners."

Ryan sighed deeply. The door to the outside kitchen filled with a big Mexican, a butcher knife in one hand and a cast-iron skillet in the other.

The Mexican's voice rang out. "No trouble in my place."

Ryan ignored him. He held his hands out at his sides, making it clear he carried no weapon, and closed the distance between himself and McGillicutty.

"You wouldn't be taking a weapon to a man with none, now, would you, Ike? A poor man weakened by that slop you call food?" he asked, his tone pleading. But as he neared the big man, he held out the quarter on the back of the fingers of his left hand, then rolled the coin across his knuckles; a faro dealer's fancy trick to pass the time.

He flipped the coin into his palm, acted as if he was flipping it away, but slid it between his fingers and showed Ike the empty hand. Ike shrugged, and Ryan neared him, then reached up and touched Ike's shirt pocket, palming the quarter again as if he was removing it from the shirt; then he held it flat in his palm, far enough away from his body that Ike's eyes strayed from his to the coin . . . and from the coming blow.

"How'd you . . . ?" Ike began.

But he didn't get the question out, as Ryan's right fist, with those rock-hard shoulders and powder-keg biceps full behind the blow, slammed into his bulbous nose, crushing it, and knocking him rolling backward into the saloon, and luckily careening the redhead back with him.

The shorter guard, Shoat, caught Ryan with a glancing right, but not before he was already coming up from the floor with a hard right uppercut, and not to the chin but to the crotch. He could tell by the man's bulging eyes and suddenly sick expression that he'd hit his target, which lifted the man in the air; then the man doubled.

The next uppercut was a left that caught the bending guard, Shoat, flush in the middle of his round face and cartwheeled him back into a table and chair.

The tall redhead recovered and came at Ryan with roundhouse punches, flailing with both arms. Ryan easily blocked them, and countered with one, two, three straight blows that snapped the man's head back and sent him stumbling over McGillicutty, who still lay prone on the saloon floor.

Ryan heard a loud command from behind him.

"Hombre!"

He turned his head just enough to catch a glance of the big Mexican proprietor and the flash of the cast-iron skillet as it smashed into the side of his head.

He went down in a heap. The last thing he remembered was doubling up in a fetal position, retching up his beefsteak, with the pounding boots of a man, or men, kicking and stomping him unmercifully.

Nico Luis Vaca rested on his veranda overlooking his high desert valley. Unseasonable thunderheads built over the canyon, which could be good news if rain actually came, and bad news if the result was nothing but the heat lightning that flashed on the horizon. North of his hacienda, above Mogollon Rim, he owned thousands of acres of forestland, ponderosa pine, where he summer-grazed his cattle and where he maintained an active lumber mill.

He fingered the paper he'd just read, then yelled over his shoulder to Magdalena, his servant woman, who was sweeping the hard earth floor of his spacious hacienda. *"Señora, donde es tá Señorita Felicia?"*

"Establo?" the woman suggested.

"Fetch her, *por favor.*"

The woman would not let him see that she was perturbed to be taken away from her chore, but she hurried away, hoping one of the vaqueros or a stable hand would be within shouting distance so she wouldn't have to waddle all the way to the barn.

For the tenth time, Vaca unfolded the paper and read the precise writing.

I received a telegram from Warden Smithson. O'Rourke is due to be released in a few days. He's not a man to turn the other cheek and as the woman is with you, I would think Rancho Conejo would be his first stop. Let us know if he drops by for a chat, or to fill your hide full of lead. It is my hope he's come to his senses and will head for California, or north. But I doubt it. I sincerely doubt it.

It was signed Leander Boyd. Lee Boyd was a partner of Nico Vaca's, a prosperous man and a prominent one, and the owner of several businesses to the north in

Prescott, the capital of the territory of Arizona.

Vaca folded the paper and stuffed it in the pocket of his *calzonevas,* the tight pants of the vaquero. He rose and walked to the rail and stood studying the several-thousand-acre land grant that was Rancho Conejo, one of four grants Vaca now owned.

But his thoughts were of Ryan O'Rourke.

"You wanted me?" a husky voice asked.

Vaca turned to see Felicia McCall standing in the doorway; stunning, even in a simple white silk blouse, red scarf tied around her fine throat, and split leather riding skirt.

"You were riding?" Vaca asked.

He was twenty years her senior, but the juices still flowed in his veins, and almost every time he eyed her, he felt heat in his loins. What a woman she was, with long auburn hair, eyes the color of dark turquoise, and skin as smooth and pure as a pail of fresh cream.

He cleared his throat, trying to keep his mind on the business at hand. He waved the message at her.

"Your old friend . . ."

She cocked her head to the side and shrugged nonchalantly.

"O'Rourke," he said.

She seemed to blanch, and then stared out over the canyon. So the man was still in her thoughts, and still had an effect on her. Vaca could feel the heat, but now in his veins. His blood suddenly ran cold, as if it were shards of ice.

Her reaction, as slight as it was, was a knife in his gut. Suddenly the sour thought came to him that when she was in his bed, she was thinking of O'Rourke. It turned his stomach, filling it with seething snakes.

"What about him?" she asked, then yawned and put the back of a fine-fingered hand to cover her mouth.

It was obvious to Vaca that it was a ploy to seem disinterested.

"He will be out of prison soon, or may be already."

"How wonderful for him," she said.

"Will he come after you?" Vaca asked, but knew the answer.

Her eyes hardened as she prepared for the lie.

"Nico, I've told you many, many times. There was nothing between Ryan and me. He was a friend, a passing acquaintance, that's all. I wish him well and hope he goes on to better his life . . . somewhere else."

Vaca smiled at her, but it was the tight-lipped grin of a viper.

"He had better, for I am judge and jury on Rancho Conejo, and in most of southern Arizona. If he comes here, he will find only the noose he should have found two years ago."

He'd goaded her, and it worked; her eyes flared and shot sparks.

"He was an innocent man and you know it. You and Polkinghorn tried to kill him, and instead he shot Polkinghorn down like the dog he was. You're lucky you're here to talk about it."

He sputtered as she walked to the rail, giving him her back. It was true, and that was the pain of it. He was shocked when O'Rourke outdrew and killed the man standing beside him. A man with so many notches on his fast gun. So shocked he hadn't been able to palm his own weapon. It was like a hot poker running down his backbone each time he thought of his cowardice, his failure to hold up his side of his bargain with Polkinghorn.

Kill O'Rourke.

O'Rourke, the acting deputy marshal of Prescott. O'Rourke, who was destroying all they'd built in the town. O'Rourke, who was organizing the merchants against him

38

and his partner, telling them the law would protect them and that they needed to pay no protection taxes to the vigilantes. A group run by Polkinghorn and Vaca. A group that no longer officially existed thanks to Ryan O'Rourke.

Even though they'd managed to pack the jury and get rid of O'Rourke for two years. But only two years, thanks to an honest federal circuit judge whom they did not own. O'Rourke would be out, and he would be back. Vaca finally managed to respond.

"You will take your supper in your room tonight, Señorita. And you will not be accompanying me to Prescott this week as planned."

"You promised I could come to see Le Commandant Cazenevue, then Caroline Richings-Bernard and *Il Trovatore.*"

Cazenevue was a magician of great reputation, and it was the only time he would be in Prescott for years to come, if ever again. And *Il Trovatore* would be at the Tempest Opera House two weeks later.

"I don't plan to stay even a full week, now that you're not accompanying me. Besides, that was before I had O'Rourke to worry about. It will be best if you stay in the safety of Rancho Conejo, with dozens of vaqueros to protect you."

She spun on her heel, her beautiful lower lip out, pouting.

"Nico, you promised. I meant nothing. . . ."

"Then you should have said nothing. You will not accompany me. Besides, there have been some cases of the diphtheria and yellow fever, and it's not safe. I would hate to lose you, *querida . . . amor.* You will remain here." He used endearments, but his tone was sarcastic.

She paused and glanced back over her shoulders.

"Why is it safe for you, *amor,* and not for me?"

"You're a woman. You are weak and must be protected."

Her eyes flared and fire lit them, but she said nothing. She stomped through the doorway and up the stairs. He could feel the whole hacienda shake as the heavy door to her room slammed.

He too stomped out to go to the *establo,* where he would undoubtedly find his *segundo,* his foreman, Montez. Only a drink of hot *pulque* would soothe his anger.

A boat? He got the impression that he was on board a swaying boat. He hadn't been shipboard even one time in his life, although he'd been on more than one riverboat, even crewed for a while on a side-wheeler on the Missouri. He was swaying gently. He tried to open his eyes, but they wouldn't open. He coughed, then realized he hurt all over; every square inch of his body, every joint, seemed sore as a boil.

Finally, he reached up and pried his right eye open with his fingers, realizing that it was swollen shut. He was swaying, but in a hammock, not a boat.

He turned his head, surveying his surroundings as well as he could with limited vision. He was in the shade of a porch, attached to a house. He heard a sound and focused on the darkness of a doorway.

A woman filled the opening, a plump but sturdy woman with a toddler resting on her hip.

"By the saints," she said, "you're alive."

"Umm," he managed through cracked and scabbed lips.

He then realized it was the miner's wife, the woman who'd given her husband such a tongue-lashing over his wanting to hire him.

She crossed the porch. "Could you take a little soup?" she asked.

He managed to nod his head, then let the swollen eye shut again, wondering how he'd manage to sit up to eat.

His question was answered for him as he heard her draw up a chair, then speak quietly.

"You lay easy and I'll spoon it in."

Her husband had been right, she wasn't much of a cook. But it was hot and laced with vegetables and small chunks of meat of some kind. Rabbit, he remembered. She continued to talk as she spooned the watery broth into him.

"Mother Mary, Jesus, and God, you caused a ruckus back there in town. As Silas would say, it got the dogs out from under the porch. Silas is in the mine and we won't see him till supper time. You been out cold for the better part of two days. A terrible beating those brutes gave you . . . a terrible beating.

"I thought sure we'd be planting you out there on the other side of the fence. Those guards are animals. They dragged you out of town and just left you lying there in the desert for the crows to pick, after they were too tired to beat you anymore.

"Silas measured your foot and your inseam, you out cold and all, and got you a pair of brogans and trousers." She laughed.

"He made that Frenchy agree that he'd take them back should you die on us."

She continued to jabber until he heard the spoon scrape the bottom of the bowl; then a child cried and he heard the chair scrape and she was gone.

In moments she was back with a wet rag, which she placed over his eyes.

"It'll help the swellin'," she said, and was gone again.

He coughed, and thought someone had shoved a hot poker between his ribs. It took him a slow count of three to catch his breath with the pain so intense.

Four

As he had done so many times the last two years when he needed solace, he centered his thoughts on Felicia. Beautiful Felicia. Those thoughts would get him through this, as they'd gotten him through the last two years.

It was hours later when he heard a man's gruff voice.

"O'Rourke, you awake?"

"If'n I wasn't, I am now."

"The missus treatin' you all right?"

Ryan managed a semblance of a smile.

"Why, yes, sir, she is. She spooned some soup down me. If you don't mind me saying so, she's as close to an angel as there is in this hellhole."

"Humph," he managed.

Then he added, "I don't believe you got anything broke. Maybe a rib . . . or more'n one. You ain't swellin' nowhere else like you would with a broke arm or leg. You'll be up and about tomorrow, God willin'."

"And weak as a kitten." It was the

woman. "Silas will be loaning you his strop and razor, should you be wantin' to be shed of that shag on your cheeks."

"I would, thank you. Soon as I can raise my arms." Ryan managed to pry open an eye. "I want you folks to know I appreciate you draggin' me up here. I probably would have died where McGillicutty and his scum left me."

"Seems to me you're tough as saddle leather," Jenkins said. Jenkins was silent for a moment.

Then, with a soft voice, he asked, "I overheard McGillicutty braggin' that you're the man who shot down Sam Polkinghorn . . . in a fair gunfight?"

"I can't deny it," Ryan managed.

"He was a feared man."

"He was. He killed a dozen men, howsome-ever most of them back-shot . . . like did most of the so-called feared gunfighters. None of 'em don't blink when a fella stands up on his hind legs and looks deep into their dirty souls," Ryan said.

"Well, sir, you're welcome here, even though we don't abide by the gun, nor killin'. We'll keep you until you can work, then as long as we can pay you, presuming you're as good with a shovel as you are with a six-gun."

"A damn sight better. I'll be ready to work in a day or so."

"A week's more like it," the woman said.

"Tomorrow," Ryan said, then added, "I remember you said the name was Jenkins?"

"That's right, Jenkins, formerly of St. Louie."

"Then thank you, Mr. and Mrs. Jenkins. I'll be in that mine with you tomorrow."

"We'll see," Jenkins said and stuck out his hand.

Ryan took it, but winced.

Jenkins continued. "By the by, I'm Silas, and this here is my wife, Sarah Ann. Out there in the garden is little Ezekial, Tobias, and Mary Beth. What's for supper," Ryan heard Silas ask as footsteps moved away.

Ryan lay quiet for a while, then realized he could see slightly out of his left eye, as the swelling was going down.

He carefully swung one leg, then the other, out of the hammock. Standing, he teetered a moment wondering if he was going to fall on his face, but managed to keep his balance.

With labored steps, he crossed the porch and leaned in the doorway.

"Here now," Sarah Ann said, "you sure you're up to this?"

"If you plan to feed me, an' I'm invited, I

46

plan to eat at the table, so as not to be more bother than need be."

"Then sit." She directed him to a chair at a table large enough for eight. He did, and in moments he had a cup of hot coffee in hand.

As she worked, she said, almost under her breath, "If you can eat, you can shave. Getting rid of that mop will make you feel better. After dinner I'll be heating you some water."

"Yes, ma'am," Ryan said with a tight smile.

Silas appeared out of an adjoining room.

"Might want to set another place. There's a wagon coming over the hill."

In a few minutes, as she brought the food to the table, Silas exited the house, then reappeared with an old man in tow.

He quickly made the introductions.

Ryan informed them that he'd met Dr. Levy on the road.

"Seem's the good doctor is a fair hand with a grinding stone," Silas said with a grin. "He's offered to sharpen all the shovels, knives, and scissors about the place in exchange for supper, breakfast, and a place in the barn."

After supper, as Ryan returned to his hammock on the porch, he was joined by

Dr. Aaron Levy and Silas, who each lit pipes. Levy offered to give Ryan a ride on to Warner's Ranch, cautioning him that he'd be stopping at every settler along the way to ply his trade.

But Ryan politely refused. "I've a debt to pay here" — then his look hardened — "and in Yuma and Prescott." The mention of those two places seemed to remind him of something, and he added, "However, I would like to take a look at that Russian you said you had for sale."

"I gave that some thought, Mr. O'Rourke, and felt I'd slighted you. A *gonnif* I'm not."

"Gonnif?" Silas asked.

"In the old language, Yiddish, a *gonnif* is a thief. To return the favor, I'll sell it for what I gave for it. Five dollars, with the re-loading tools and two dozen rounds, since you helped me on the road and took nothing but a smile and a thank-you."

"Is there a holster and belt?" Ryan asked, scratching his head.

"Now it's you should worry about being the *gonnif.*"

Ryan laughed. "If it's tight, you've got a deal." He extended his hand, but winced with the old man's hard grip on his swollen knuckles.

Silas eyed them both skeptically, but said nothing.

After going to his wagon and fetching the weapon, Levy returned with both the weapon and a fiddle. He sat by the hammock and explained the weapon in detail, as Ryan handled it with swollen hands, breaking it repeatedly with the barrel and cylinder falling away and admiring the ejectors.

"It's a Model 3 American, single-action, self-ejecting, .45-caliber with a four-inch barrel and carved bone grips, made in 1870, so it's something over seven years old," Levy said.

"I imagine it's a Union Cavalry weapon gone astray, as it's stamped U.S. It's been fancied up a mite since the army claimed it, with its carved bone grips and all," Ryan said.

"The short barrel makes it easy to pull, should a fella have need for hurry-up. All in all, she's *balebatish*."

Ryan smiled. "I imagine that's grand, or cheap, or some such?"

"Or some such," Levy said, grinning.

When they returned to the porch, Sarah Ann was waiting with a bone-white bowl of hot water, a strop, a razor, and a mug of soap.

Ryan felt like a human for the first time in a long while after he shed the long whiskers. When he was finished, Sarah Ann reappeared in the doorway, scissors in hand.

"Would you trust me to cut that mop?"

He smiled and nodded.

When she was finished, she stood back, hands on ample hips, and eyed her work critically.

"By all that's holy, under all that hair was a fine-looking man."

"Would you mind if I play?" Levy asked, picking up the fiddle.

"I love a fiddle," Ryan said.

"This, sir, is a violin," Levy informed them.

In moments, the old man had them all in tears, so beautiful was his playing.

After breakfast the next morning, and after sharpening all the shovels, knives, and Sarah Ann's scissors, and pocketing five of Ryan's remaining dollars, Levy whipped up his mules.

Ryan was beginning to be partial to the old man, and was sorry to see him go.

Over the next week, Ryan regained his strength. At first, he was merely handing tools to Silas, then managing to push the ore cart out of the mine, then, finally, on the fifth day, he was swinging a pick and shoveling.

"I'll be paying you half wages up to today. From now on, it's a dollar a day and found."

"Fair enough," Ryan said. "I'll give you a month; then I'll have enough to buy a nag or for stage fare back to Prescott."

"A month, if that's all you've got to give."

"I've got business, Silas. A month it is."

"By the look of you when you talk of it, I'd say it's the devil's business?"

"Could be, but it's got to be done if I'm ever to have some peace."

"A man deserves to find some of that rare commodity." Silas finally smiled.

"Then let's make the best of it," Ryan said with a determined glance, and went back to swinging the pick at a quicker pace.

Had Ryan not been two years at hard labor, he would have folded under the pace and heat. Luckily, it was fifteen degrees cooler in the mine, but still it must have been near one hundred degrees.

They worked six and a half days a week for the next month. Ryan kept careful track. At supper on the thirtieth day, rabbit stew and dumplings, Ryan announced he

51

was leaving. Silas retired to the couple's bedroom and returned with a pouch. He carefully counted out the thirty-six dollars and fifty cents.

With that done, Ryan walked to the doorway, then suggested, "I'd like to talk to you about that dun gelding in the corral, and your spare tack." It was a spare horse, one of five that Silas kept. He needed two to make a team for the wagon, and two to ride. It wasn't a particularly handsome horse, other than its color, a buttermilk dun. Its light color would help it stand up to the desert sun.

"I could up your pay to a dollar and a half a day."

"Dollar was fair enough, Silas. That's not a consideration."

"You wait a few months and you'll be able to take the train to Los Angeles, or even San Francisco, and you'll have the money, me paying you a buck and a half. The railroad's only a few dozen miles northwest from Yuma, and building fast."

"I'm going the other way."

"You sure you want that mustang? It's only eight miles to Yuma," Silas said, his eyes narrowing, immediately falling into a bargaining mode.

"And two hundred or more to Prescott,"

Ryan countered. "Besides, you're just eatin' up what little pasture there is hereabout keeping a horse you don't need. I'd be doing you a favor taking that killer off your hands."

"Killer! Why, that horse is a lover. Gentle as a morning breeze."

"Hurricane, you mean."

Both of them laughed.

As Sarah cleared the table, Silas and Ryan walked out to the corral, leaned on the top rail, and eyed the horse. Silas fetched a saddle and bridle and threw it over the rail. It was July and the metal bit was hot to the touch, even though it had been resting in the shade, and the saddle was in need of a good tallowing.

"Hell's fire," Silas said, "I'd give you the loan of him to Yuma if it's the walk concerns you. Talbot's Livery will have a half dozen horses to sell, broke so as your grandma could ride them."

After a half hour of haggling, of saddling and riding the rank animal around the corral, Ryan — eighteen dollars poorer — was the proud owner of a semi-tame but strong fifteen-hand dun gelding, with blanket, McClellan saddle, albeit one with a few cracks, and bridle with a spade bit. The saddle carried the original canteen, picket pin, and hemp lead rope, nose bag with blanket, and military rifle saddle scabbard — a small sheath two hand-breadths long, designed to hold an army-issue Springfield carbine, although Ryan had no rifle to fill it.

To his pleasure, by stuffing the barrel hole with a rag, he discovered that the Russian model fit nicely into the device. So he had a fancy brass-trimmed saddle holster.

When Ryan was ready, Silas extended his hand. "You'd be a wiser man to ride north along the Colorado, then follow the Virgin up through its canyon, then due north along the west slope of the Wasatch. The Mormons are a hard but fair folk, but they'll have work for you. Before the snow flies, you can be with your family in Montana."

"I'm sure you're right, Silas, but there's business in Yuma and Prescott."

"McGillicutty and that bunch have made their hell on earth and they'll suffer even more in the beyond. I can't speak for your Prescott trouble. *If* you get to Prescott. Rumor is, in the year and a half since the Custer massacre, the Indians all over the West are feeling their oats. The Mojaves, Maricopas, and Pimas are raising hell, and the Apaches have been known to wander far enough northwest to cause you trouble dang near anywheres along the Gila."

"Silas, you're doing your damnedest to convince me to stay."

Silas smiled sheepishly. "You're a good hand, and the family's taken a fancy to you."

Ryan grinned. "And I to them. But everything in its time, Silas. I'll worry about the redskins when it's their time. And as to McGillicutty making his own hell on earth . . . it's a shady walk by the river compared to the hell I'm sending him to."

Ryan swung up into the saddle, and as usual the horse shied away as he was mounting, but Ryan got him forked and quieted him.

"I appreciate the work, Silas," he said. "You're a hell of a hand and you have a fine handsome family."

"Hold up a minute," Silas said, jogging to the house. When he came out, he had the whole family with him.

Ryan owed Sarah Ann for her kindness, but he hated good-byes. He'd grown particularly fond of the oldest boy, Ezekiel, having spent a great deal of his time off with him.

Silas stood on the porch that had become Ryan's home for the past month. He had an old wide-brimmed hat in hand. He handed it to Zeke, whispered to him, and the boy scampered off the porch and ran over, handing it up to Ryan.

"Papa says you'll need this for the crossing. Man shouldn't be without a hat. Says it'll fry your brain if'n you got no hat, and" — he laughed — "and if the redskins scalp you, Pa says it'll cover up the bald spot."

"Thank you. You take care of your ma and pa and the little ones, Zeke."

"Yes, sir. Mr. O'Rourke, thanks for teaching me all them knots and how to braid horsehair."

Ryan smiled and nodded, then tipped the hat to Sarah Ann.

"Miss Sarah, I'd climb down from here and give you a hug that would take your breath, if'n your old man wasn't so big, ugly, and tough."

She laughed as he whipped up the horse, who humped a couple of times trying to shed himself of the man, then settled and clattered out down the long, dry canyon, lined with deer-horn cactus and Joshua trees, toward the river four miles below.

A horned toad scampered out from the shade of a rock near the trail, glared at him, then disappeared into a creosote bush; a turkey vulture circled high above; and a small herd of desert bighorn watched him from a distant cliff-side canyon wall — but after he was out of sight of the mine, they were the only signs of life.

He had money in his pocket, a horse and sidearm, a blanket and near-waterproof nose bag that would double to haul water should any be found, and a canteen full of fresh well water.

He was far better off than he had been when he got out of the hellhole. But there was still hard business in Yuma.

The man who'd beaten and degraded him in prison, a man who he was sure had stolen most of the hundred dollars he had hidden in a cleft of the rock, a carefully hollowed-out joint between stones, at the level of his bunk.

A man who'd used a club and hard-toed boots on him, while he was being held by other cowards; a man who'd left him for dead after he'd served his time.

Iron Ike McGillicutty.

Five

Ryan reined up alongside the river in the shade of a pair of smoke trees. The sun was directly overhead, so it was noon or near to it. He had business in town other than McGillicutty, so he decided to ride on in, then out again before the big guard took his leave of the prison after the day's work and headed for Ramon's Saloon and Restaurant.

It wasn't that he didn't want to face the big guard — in fact that was exactly what he was here for — but if the man was with Parsons and Shott, and he normally hung with those two, Ryan knew he'd have to have an edge.

He'd learned after a few years as a deputy marshal that having an edge often meant the difference between life and death. And the only edge he could figure on having was leaving the three men bending elbows at the plank bar for a good while before he came to call . . . to make his play. They seemed the type to drink at least a bottle of whiskey between them, maybe two. That was the edge he needed.

One thing he was sure of. He wanted witnesses, lots of witnesses, and he wanted to make sure that McGillicutty made the first move.

It would be a fair fight, but the last fair fight had cost him two years in jail. He wouldn't wait around for a hearing this time, but he'd light a shuck out knowing he'd been on the side of right . . . whatever good that might do him.

Ryan rode on in and tied the mustang up in front of Andre's Mercantile and Dry Goods.

Knowing he had to stretch the money in his pocket, he was careful about what he took to the counter, where a small, sallow-faced man with a heavy accent kept the tab.

"Let's see," the man, who Ryan presumed was Andre, said. "A pound of Arbuckle's, two pounds of biscuits, a slab of bacon, a box of fifty-count .45-caliber cartridges, a two-gallon water bag, one cotton shirt size extra-large, a six-foot-by-ten-foot square of Goodrich's tent cloth, needle and a spool of thread, six ounces of salt, twenty feet of fine hemp line, a bottle of Holseadters Bitters, a two-inch-by-eight-foot strip of tanned bull hide, and a fine skinning knife. That's . . . let me see . . . that'll be five dollars and eighty-five cents."

Ryan had watched carefully as the man totaled the sum, then counted out the money.

He looked around to make sure no one else was in the store, then whipped off the rag that was his prison shirt.

"Can't interest you in a bottle of good whiskey?" Andre asked. "Fifty cents."

"No, sir, I'm headed for the railhead, then on to Los Angeles."

He purposely lied to the man as he buttoned the new shirt. "I imagine everything will be cheaper in the company store there."

"Humph," the Frenchman said. "I wouldn't count on it."

"I will take two of these," he said, reaching deep into a big bottle that rested on the counter. He fished out two pieces of rock candy and placed a penny on the counter.

Ryan left, goods in hand, untied the dun, and led it to the livery, which doubled as a blacksmith shop. He had the bag of goods slung over his shoulder.

"You Dutch?" he asked a big barrel-chested man with straw-colored hair who stood, hammer and tongs in hand, in front of a bellows and fire.

The man turned and eyed Ryan.

"I am. Dutch Vanderbeck." He mopped his brow, streaked with carbon and sweat, as he spoke.

"How much to shoe the dun?"

"Dollar should do it."

"I'd hope so. How about half that?"

The big man smiled sardonically. "It's only seventy-five miles to the next smithy. Maybe you'd like to get another bid, if'n that crow-bait will get you there."

Ryan smiled and shrugged. "Give me a full dollar's worth, and a spare shoe and a few nails for the trail, and it's a deal."

"Dollar and a dime," Dutch said, and went back to pounding on the gate hasp that had his attention.

"Fair enough, but I need it done right away."

He wanted to make sure he was out of town well before six o'clock, quitting time at the prison.

"Let's see your money," Dutch said.

"You're a trusting sort," Ryan said with some sarcasm.

"I saw you up in the castle when I was there doing some work on the cell doors.

You got arms like a blacksmith, but I still wouldn't think you'd be the best risk."

Ryan reached in his pocket and showed the smith his money.

"You paying in advance?" Dutch asked.

"Nope. You do a job of work, you'll get your money."

He turned, walked over, sat on a bale of hay, and watched as the smith fought the rank dun to get a hoof lifted and trimmed. Finally, Dutch stomped over to a storeroom and came out with a feed bag and blindfolded the animal.

Ryan sat on the bale, not offering to help, or even to hold and calm the horse.

It took the better part of a half hour, but finally Dutch walked over and held out his hand, palm up.

Ryan counted out a dollar and a dime, and the man turned to walk back to his bellows.

"Nice job. Worth the money," Ryan admitted, then asked, "You got three or four mules out in your corral?"

"I do. Fine animals."

"Them what's for sale always are, in the eye of the seller. How much for the pick of the litter?"

"Twenty dollars will buy any one of them. Twelve might buy the runt, but I'll warn you, he's mean enough to steal eggs from a widow woman's henhouse and cunning enough to hide the shells under the neighbor's porch."

As much as Ryan was beginning to dislike the Dutchman, that one made him smile.

"I don't have twenty dollars left. I could part with nine . . . but that's the best I can do. But I'd take that devil mule off your hands."

"Then I guess you won't be having a mule." Dutch turned back to his work.

"You owe me a shoe and a handful of nails."

The man dug in his leather apron and handed him the merchandise without speaking, then went back to shaping the hasp.

Ryan walked over and mounted the dun, who stood quiet for a change, seemingly happy that he wasn't being hoof-hoisted and pounded on. Tying the sack full of goods behind the saddle, Ryan gigged the animal back toward the river, where he planned to find a shady spot and wait the rest of the afternoon out.

Captain Leander Boyd had come to Prescott in the late sixties like most, following the rumors of gold in every canyon. He was fresh out of the Union army, and ready to make his fortune.

He'd earned a field commission of captain — a result of his becoming a lieutenant when he managed to flee the approaching force of Brigadier General Nathan Bedford Forest at Murfreesboro, Tennessee, then getting promoted again. Normally, fleeing an approaching force would not be the meat of a field commission, but Boyd, an infantryman with the 9th Pennsylvania, fled after requisitioning a dozen farm mules and dragging a half dozen six-pounders behind. About all that was saved when Forest's men overran the Union supply center on the Nashville & Chattanooga Railroad.

His own general, Thomas T. Crittenden, field-promoted him from a lowly corporal to sergeant to lieutenant as a result, then later to captain.

He hadn't been uncommonly brave, but he had been cunning, which made up for it.

Unfortunately, after the war ended, Boyd had no family business to return to, nor even a job. Before being conscripted he'd been a clerk in ship's chandlery, and his position had long been filled.

Instead of heading back to Pennsylvania, he headed west, intent on having his fortunes rise in business as they had in war.

After a little over ten years, Boyd owned ten businesses in the thriving town and capital of the territory of Arizona, Prescott. Two saloons and gambling houses, the Sundown and Suzzette's; the Tempest Opera House; the Palace, a three-story, twenty-four-room hotel; Boyd's, a mercantile fashioned much after the chandlery; a livery that housed one of two stage companies and the territorial post office; a pair of Chinese joss houses complete with fat Buddha statuary and opium dens; and a pair of brothels.

He also owned three farms in the Cottonwood Valley, each of which was operated by a Chinese partner, a Celestial — a partner in the operation, but not in the ownership of the land. He'd found the Chinese to be honest and dependable, and it was advantageous that legally they couldn't own land. They were partners over whom he held a large hammer, a situation he savored.

Boyd was a silent partner in the *Miner's Gazette*, a weekly paper, and in a number of mines. He enjoyed not having anything negative said about him in the local paper, and its ability to sway opinion regarding other matters of importance, but he stayed out of the limelight as an independent opinion was far more highly valued.

He also had a partner in both the saloons and the brothels, Don Nico Luis Vaca.

Vaca had been the most powerful man in the territory long before it was a territory, having inherited a land grant from his father, and quadrupling its size by acquiring two more grants north of the border and one south.

His holdings were well over 100,000 acres, and even he didn't know how many cattle grazed his land.

The most profitable venture for them had been the Territorial Vigilante Committee, until that scheme had been discovered and exposed by Deputy Marshal Ryan O'Rourke. The Irishman had been a rare sort, a man who couldn't be bought or even manipulated.

The vigilantes had been disbanded by the new governor, John Fremont, when O'Rourke brought him a handful of depositions from local businesses and mines that testified to the fact they were paying the "committee" for protection.

Even Boyd and Vaca didn't want to go

up against the popular Fremont, who was seemingly as incorruptible as O'Rourke.

Boyd nervously bit the end off his cigar, then scratched a match and lit it. He was not a man given to nervousness, and it irritated him. He left his office in the hotel and stomped across to the opera house, entered, and went straight to the small office off the lobby.

McManus Peters, the Eastern man he'd hired to manage the enterprise, a retired actor who'd never been particularly successful, was at his desk, reading a copy of *Leslie's.* He looked up to see his boss at his door and made no effort to hide the paper.

Keeping up with popular plays, shows, circuses, and lecturers was part of his job.

"We might get Dr. Horace Cromwell to come in for a lecture series," he said without greeting Boyd.

"He's the geologist and anthropologist?"

"Trained as a geologist, and an amateur — if accomplished amateur — anthropologist."

"For a percentage of the take?"

"I telegrammed him the first of the week. He wants a two-hundred-dollar guarantee against half the house."

"For how many lectures?"

"Three nights. One on the origin of gold and silver, one on lead, and one on the origin of the human species."

"Do as you want, but be right. Sounds like it would appeal mostly to the miners, and you've got to get them into town."

"Which will make you money in the hotel and saloons. How the hell can you be right all the time in this business?"

"The house is dark for the next four days?" Boyd asked.

"It's a few days before Cromwell could get here. He's in Denver. And then more than a week until Richings-Bernard and *Il Trovatore* will begin. What do you need?" Cromwell asked, knowing his boss was about to request something apart from the theater.

"How many of the old vigilante committee is around?"

"Maxwell and Higginbottom left the country, but the rest are still in pocket. A half dozen or so."

"Set up a meeting here tonight. We'll supply the whiskey. I might have a job of work for the likes of them."

"What time?"

"Make it nine. All those who aren't working in some saloon or brothel should be available. Parkinson and Holstadt are

68

working for me at the Silver Dollar and I'll let them know. You locate the others."

"What's up?"

"O'Rourke."

"The former deputy marshal?"

"One and the same."

"I thought he was bustin' rocks. A guest of the territory in Yuma."

"He's out."

Six

It was dark when Ryan pulled a couple of biscuits from the tin he'd bought and munched on them. They weren't much after Sarah Ann's fresh biscuits and jam. She'd turned out to be a much better cook than Silas had said.

He'd spent the afternoon practicing pulling the Russian from his belt. Early on he had fired it a half dozen times at an old peach tin he'd placed in the crouch of a mesquite, hitting it twice from twenty-five paces. Old man Levy had done right by him as it was a good weapon. The other four shots had been close enough that it would discourage anything the size of a man. And the .45 had stopping power, with a slug the size of the last digit of your little finger. You wouldn't have to hit the average man twice with a pea from this shooter. If you hit big bone, it would knock him ass over teakettle, and the odds were he wouldn't be getting up again.

He decided he'd waited long enough.

After brushing the dun the best he could with his hand, he saddled and mounted.

As usual, the horse pitched a few times, but settled.

He was less than a quarter mile from town, and rode it at a slow walk.

There was only one building with light in the windows, and that was Ramon's. Ryan was not surprised to see that the big Dutchman was still working at his bellows by lantern light — obviously he was a single man.

A half dozen horses were tied at Ramon's rail. He hoped they weren't all cronies of McGillicutty's. He tied the dun off to the side, away from the other horses. If he had to mount quickly, he didn't want to have to fight his way between strange horses.

Moving quietly across the plank boardwalk, he paused at the batwing doors and studied the inside. As he'd expected, McGillicutty was there, but not standing at the bar with Shott and Parsons. He was at a table playing poker, his back to the doors, the club hanging at his side, his converted Colt revolver on the other.

Ryan knew that revolver well as he'd tasted its steel more than once. He recognized the prison warden, Tobias Smithson, who was also in the game; and the Frenchman, Andre, from the mercantile. Three other men who looked like miners or freighters sat at the table, and two men stood at the bar in addition to McGillicutty's cronies, but they stood at the end to themselves.

The big Mexican, whom Ryan guessed was Ramon, tended bar. Ryan presumed his cook duties were finished for the night, so he'd taken over where the real money was.

Ryan pulled the Russian from his belt a couple of times to make sure it would jerk without hanging up.

Satisfied, Ryan took a deep breath, then quietly pushed into the room. Smoke hung low, almost occluding the sculptured tin ceiling.

The bartender seemed to be the only one who noticed him, and he stopped polishing a mug and eyed Ryan skeptically. But Ryan was clean-shaven with miner's brogans, trousers, and one of Silas's old shirts.

Ryan saw no reason to let everyone know he was there and put them on notice, so he walked directly over to take a position a half dozen steps behind McGillicutty, where he could still see Parsons and Shott at the bar.

He let his voice ring across the saloon.

"Ike, you offal-eatin' pig, let's see how good your club is working today, and if it's any good against this Russian I'm toting."

The room quieted. McGillicutty seemed to stiffen. Then Ryan heard him chuckle.

"I'll raise you a quarter," Ike said, eyeing a man across the table, seemingly ignoring the threat behind him. He had several gold and silver coins stacked on the table in front of him.

The warden, Smithson, rose to his feet, hands out to his side, showing he was unarmed.

The warden glowered at Ryan over his handlebar mustache.

"You look like a man just dying to get back into the castle."

"Nope, just trying to right a wrong."

"There are a half dozen witnesses here, Ryan."

"I was counting on it, Warden. Me shooting this pile of pig shit fulla holes is gonna be self-defense. McGillicutty is a cowardly cur who won't face a man head-to-head. He's got to have help. I want these men to see what a low-life snake he is, even though they already know it to be true. I truly believe his mama was a New Hampshire hog and his daddy a butt-lickin' cur."

Ryan stepped forward and kicked the bottom of Ike's chair.

"Stand up, Fat Ike," Ryan demanded, "and fill your hand."

He could see Ike stiffen, but the big man left his hands flat on the table and didn't move.

"You'll hang, if you live," Smithson said, but he backed a couple of steps away from the table. The three miners rose and followed his lead, going all the way to the bar. The Frenchman almost ran to follow, knocking a chair over as he leapt to his feet and bolted.

"Warden, this is gonna be a fair fight, and you're gonna witness it," Ryan said.

Out of the corner of his eye, Ryan could see that Ramon, the bartender, was fishing under the bar for something.

"Mexican," Ryan snapped, "I got an itch to shoot you into a pile of enchilada meat for that frying pan upside my head.

"I was damn near beat to death 'cause of you. You come up with a scattergun, you better be quicker than a sixteen-year-old in a French whorehouse . . . you're about to die fast and first."

The Mexican raised both his hands and, wide-eyed, backed away until he was up against the back bar.

Both Parsons and Shott were wearing sidearms, and both were facing Ryan with their hands at the ready.

"And Shoat," Ryan said, purposefully insulting the man, "I got plenty of undeserved knots from you and Parsons. I didn't come here to kill you two, but I'll be happy to accommodate, you give me a flea's dick more cause."

Ryan moved a couple of steps closer to the wall, so he was positioned to better see both McGillicutty and the bar.

Without lifting his hands off the table, McGillicutty looked back over his shoulder.

"O'Rourke, I got to get up and turn around."

"Back away, Warden," Ryan said. "I don't want you should get hit by a stray, even though you condone what goes on it that hellhole."

Ryan's voice lowered. "Say a quick prayer, then get on your feet, Ike."

It was so quiet in the bar you could hear the bubbles break in the beer foam.

Ike rose, still without lifting his hands from the table, slipping the chair back with the back of his legs as he did so.

"It don't have to be this way, O'Rourke," he said.

"I guess it don't, Ike. You can pay me

back the gold coin you stole from me and we can go out in the street, me with that knotheaded club I've come to know so well — give me the loan of it and I can beat on you a while. A damn long while.

"If you live, after I break every bone in your sorry body, you'll not be able to mistreat another prisoner. We can do that, if you'd prefer."

"I'm turning around," Ike said, his voice low and raspy.

"I was counting on it."

As he slowly turned, he called out to his friends at the bar. "Parsons, Shott, you backing me up?"

He didn't get an answer.

He glowered at Ryan, standing with the firearm still in his belt.

"Hell, man," Ike said with a guffaw, "you don't even have that little pissant thing in hand. I'm obliged to kill you where you stand."

"Then get on with it, Fat Ike," Ryan growled.

It was hot as Hades in the place, and the sweat was running down Ike's forehead.

He glared at Ryan for a minute, then spat on the floor. "Are you sure —"

"You draw, or I will," Ryan said.

Before he finished, Ike reached.

Ryan's shot was first and chest-high, and as he figured, when he hit bone, Ike flew backward across the table, but not before getting a shot off that creased Ryan's outer thigh. Other men dove for the floor, trying to get out of the line of fire. A couple of the miners ran for the doors, and the bartender hit the floor behind the bar.

Ryan slammed his own back against the wall, seeing Shott leveling his Colt at him.

Ryan fired at the same time Shott did, then fired again as Shott didn't drop the gun, but bounced off the bar and stared down at his bloodied chest.

With the second slug Shott was slammed against the bar, then pitched forward on his face.

Parsons, eyes wide, had his hands in the air.

"You kilt 'em, you kilt 'em both," Parsons stammered.

"And I'd be pleased to accommodate you, old son."

The air was acrid with gun smoke.

The table that Ike was lying across slowly collapsed to the floor, and Ike rolled away. His eyes were open, unmoving, his chest had a gaping wound, but the blood had stopped pumping.

Blood reddened the side of Ryan's thigh

from Ike's wild shot and ran down the side of his face from a half circle cut in his ear by Shott's slug.

"Self-defense," Ryan snapped as he swept the room with his weapon.

But neither the warden nor anyone said a word.

"Warden!" Ryan growled.

"Well, you didn't draw first. A jury might see it that way. But this wouldn't have happened had you rode away."

"It wouldn't have happened had you been watchin' the goings-on in that pigsty you call a prison."

Money was scattered all over the floor. Ryan knelt, keeping his eyes and muzzle scanning the men. "Smithson, how much money did Ike have on the table?"

"Hell, I don't know."

"Guess."

"Fifty, maybe sixty dollars."

"He owes me the better part of a hundred." He found a pair of twenty-dollar gold pieces and a ten-dollar one, and rose as he pocketed them. "That's owed, that was stole from me. I'm no thief."

Ryan backed toward the door. He paused in the doorway. "That's Ike's roan outside?"

"It is," Smithson said.

"Anybody want to buy it?" Ryan asked, but as he surmised, he got no answer.

"I'm going out now. I got a little business here in town. I wouldn't be sticking my ugly head out if I was you boys, until you hear my hoofbeats leaving this pigsty you call a town."

No one replied as Ryan swept the room with the muzzle of the Russian one more time.

He backed through the door, then turned and saw a big man in the road, and snapped the Russian up again.

The big Dutchman must have heard the gunfire, and was standing as if he couldn't make up his mind about going inside, the light from the saloon reflecting in his straw-colored hair, his hands up, palms out as if he could ward off shots from the Russian.

"You're just the man I wanna see," Ryan said.

"Why's that?" he asked, looking apprehensive.

"You got a packsaddle for that mule?"

"I do, with canvas bags and panniers."

"Will you throw them in for that twenty you're asking?"

"I will," he sputtered. "They ain't much."

Ryan flipped him one of the twenties. "Then get him rigged and ready."

Since he would have the mule, he turned and went back to the batwings and stood looking over them as he spoke to the men gathered around McGillicutty and Shott.

"Frenchy!" he yelled at the merchantile owner.

The man rose from a kneeling position beside Shott and stared at him.

"I'd appreciate it if you'd open up for a minute."

Frenchy looked around, hoping someone would make Ryan disappear.

"I won't be taking much of your time, and I got cash money."

Andre moved forward quickly, and Ryan stepped aside and let him pass. He turned back to the doors and yelled to those inside the again-silent saloon.

"I'm gonna have a scattergun in hand and any man in the street will be splattered to the wind when I come out. Go back to yer beers."

Passing Ike's roan, Ryan eyed him carefully, then decided against taking the big horse. They would consider him a horse thief, and folks would condemn a horse thief even more than a murderer in most of the West, where a horse could mean life or death.

He followed Andre to his store. Leading the dun and tying him outside, he went in and quickly assembled the goods he'd need, including another two-gallon canteen and a frying pan. He traded his well-broken-in brogans for a pair of heeled riding boots and bought some bull-hide chaps for brush-bustin' the desert.

When he paid and exited the store, the mule was tied in front of the livery, saddled and ready to go.

Ryan quickly rolled his goods in a new canvas, threw them over the packsaddle, tied them in place, and in moments rode north out of town as if he were crossing the river. Instead, he rode only a few feet into the stream, careful of the quicksand for which the river was famous.

He followed the Colorado upstream for a few hundred yards, then moved out into a copse of willows and headed for the Gila River, which would lead him east, into the desert, to Prescott, to Vaca, Boyd, Parkinson, and Holstadt, the no-good lying cheats who'd taken all he had . . . stolen all he had, all he was.

When he finished with them, he'd find Felicia.

He didn't buy a scattergun as he'd threatened he would to those in the saloon; he'd gone one better.

A shiny new Winchester 73 was now shoved in the saddle scabbard.

Seven

He'd let the dun find his own way a few miles into the Sonoran Desert, roughly following the Gila River — which was only an occasional sink here this time of year, most of it only a dry bed of sand and gravel — until well after midnight.

The bad news was his leg was aching badly from the crease and burn of Shott's bullet, and it hadn't stopped weeping.

The notch in his ear had quit bleeding, but its bullet-sculpted odd shape wouldn't help his already dubious looks. The good news was a three-quarter waxing moon in a clear sky to light the way, and the nighttime desert coolness. Figuring he was eight or nine miles from Yuma, he finally reined up, unsaddled, rubbed down and staked the dun and mule, and using the saddle for a pillow, slept the rest of the short night away.

The old Butterfield stage road, currently the route of the Tucson-Los Angeles Express and the wire, along the south side of the river, would have been much easier, but much more risky.

The stage stops lay fifteen to twenty miles apart, dictated mostly by a spring or stand of cottonwood, or infrequent sinks in the river. News of the trouble in Yuma would travel fast along the stage route, and a couple of the stage stops now had the wire to forward messages. And if he was a wanted man, stationmasters would know it as quickly as anyone.

In fact, they probably already did.

No, stage stops were out of the question until he knew the outcome of his recent activities. He knew he'd be wanted for a hearing at least, but it was the outcome of that hearing he was worried about.

He was satisfied he'd clearly acted in self-defense, as the others had reached for their weapons first, but eyesight and recollection are the handmaidens of friendship, relations, and old debts. He counted on Ike being almost as disliked by townspeople as he was by inmates, if that could be possible.

He didn't know about Shott.

But he did know neither of them were married men. If Ike and Shott were disliked, a hearing would result in no arraignment, no wanted posters, no reward. If not, then it would follow him, hunt him, haunt him.

Dawn across the desert can be spectacular, and this morning's was all of that. And his leg had scabbed over and quit bleeding. It would most likely break open while he was in the saddle, dodging prickly pear, barrel and rainbow cactus, and pounding across sand, stone, and gravel. However, a clear sky and temperatures already quickly climbing portended what was to face him.

Had it not been for the mess he'd left behind, and the potential of a posse, he would have found a shady cliff side or cut in the riverbank and lain up until nightfall, but that wasn't to be. Maybe tomorrow.

As the sky went from orange to lemon yellow, he made coffee and had a few of the biscuits. He'd staked the buttermilk dun and black mule in a patch of drying grass in reach of a patch of greasewood, which he knew sheep would eat and which he hoped would feed the horse and mule.

The sun was just over the rocky peaks to the east when he set out at a steady walk. He wanted the dun ready to run should he sight a posse behind him, and it wouldn't do to push him too hard, particularly in the growing heat. A dozen or so miles in the distance, he could see the bright red mountain that was Pringle's Peak, and he knew that Texas Hill was nearby.

A stage station was located there, because of sinks in the nearby bed of the Gila. It was the only water he was positive of in this first day, and he had to get the animals there.

In the desert, do what you can, and what won't kill you, the old sergeant had taught him. His first goal was Texas Hill, and the sinks.

By the time he reached the sinks in late afternoon, the horse was lathered even though never pushed beyond a walk; the mule was in better shape, but with a desert donkey in his ancestry, that was to be expected, and Ryan was dehydrated and tasting dirt, unable to make spit.

He'd given the dun three-quarters of the water in his canteens during the hot ride, and only wet his and the mule's lips. Had he been carrying the horse, he would have drunk deeply.

They found the most distant sink from the station, a muddy hole surrounded by yellow: pepper grass and the remnants of sulfur flowers. Beyond, it was sheltered by a copse of blue paloverde trees and cat-claw.

He was well out of sight of the stage station. While he watered the horse and himself with the gritty water, he heard the stage rattle past, and the encouragement of the stage driver as he shouted at the team.

Hundreds of tiny pupfish darted in and out of sight in the muddy water, but they weren't worth expending the effort to catch, even if he could. It would take a half dozen to make a bite. However, he wished he had a scattergun and was out of earshot of the stage station, as by the time he saddled up, hundreds of white-wing and a few mourning doves were visiting the sinks for their nightly drink, and a covey of quail whistled in the background.

It was a feast, but it might as well have been sitting on a table in Paris for all the good it did him.

He passed the time by cutting a piece of the tent cloth and wrapping his leg, to try and get the weeping to stop. The ear had scabbed over and would heal, but he worried about the groove in his thigh going green on him.

They'd rested for an hour. He thought of a hot meal at the station, but it was out of the question. He wanted to be well away from the stage station before he made camp for the night, as he didn't want his smoke seen. He'd been dreaming of coffee and frying bacon and biscuits soaked in bacon grease all day — when he wasn't dreaming of fresh cold water.

Five or six miles later, just as it was beginning to be too dark to see, the waxing moon rose larger than last night. He could ride on, but decided rest and sustenance more important.

Making a dry camp in the sandy Gila bed, below a line of smoke trees topping a deep cut made by the river, he drank his fill before watering the horse with one of the canteens and the mule with the other and staking them in some dried grass where they could reach a few large greasewood shrubs, carefully keeping the horse short enough that he couldn't reach a clump of snakeweed, toxic to horses.

The mule, he knew, was desert-wise enough to fend for himself. But all in all, what they had was poor fodder.

The old sergeant had told him of a water hole a couple of miles south of the river, a spring-fed hole surrounded by a grove of crucifixion thorn trees, on the very edge of Oatman Flats, more than a mile from the Oatman Flats Stage Station.

The flats got their name as a result of being the burial place of the Oatmans, killed by Apaches who absconded with their two daughters, leaving the parents and a brother for dead.

The brother survived by crawling for miles even though badly wounded, and went on to later rescue one of his sisters, although the other died in captivity.

Oatman Flats was twenty-two miles of arid plain, ending near Dutchman's Station, another stage stop.

The biscuits and bacon were the stuff of dreams, and he slept well under a blanket of stars that it seemed he could reach out and touch, with the hard silhouetted shoulders of rocky mountain ridges in the distance.

As soon as the bacon fat cooled, he used the remnants to grease his lips, which were already dry and brittle. In the morning, he decided, he'd place a gob in his shirt pocket, to keep his lips from cracking and bleeding.

He awoke late, but still before the sun was full over the mountains to the east. Serenaded by a pair of northern flickers and their piercing calls, he arose to quickly rub down the animals, pack the mule, and saddle the dun. It would be a drink of water and one bacon grease soaked biscuit that he'd saved, and only a quarter canteen of water for the dun.

He had to find the spring-fed pool the old man had described.

It took him almost an hour to find the water hole, which the old man had told him was surrounded by thorn-covered crucifixion trees. What he didn't mention was the fact that it was in a deep arroyo almost to the edge of a rocky ridge of limestone.

Ryan finally had to depend on an old Indian trick of following bees, cliff swallows after the mud, and white-wing doves looking for their morning drink.

He found a game trail down the cliff side, covered with deer and desert bighorn sheep tracks, and let the animals water and graze on poolside grass for another thirty minutes, risking the higher temperatures because he wasn't willing to attempt the flats with the animals underfed.

While the animals grazed, he climbed high on the cliff face, studying his back trail; still no sign of pursuers.

Behind him, in the country he'd crossed, the desert was towering saguaro, Joshua trees, mesquite, and a variety of cactus, yucca, and sage; but in front, it was sand and pebble plain with only the occasional creosote, greasewood, or snakeweed. It would be a hard twenty-two miles, but not as hard as the flats beyond — forty miles of alkali with only a few stands of coarse grass.

Maricopa Flats, hell on earth.

Even the stage companies changed their horse teams to mules to cross the Maricopa, as horses couldn't stand the grueling, waterless pace.

He let the dun set his own gait, which was a comfortable lope for the first three or four miles, until the heat slowed him to a walk. When Ryan figured they were a little more than a third of the way across the flats, he reined up and watered the dun from a canteen using the nose bag, and even spared the tough mule a pint.

Finally, in the early afternoon, just a little more than halfway, they came upon a grove of smoke trees offering a little shade, and he decided to rest and water with the rest of his canteens through the heat of the afternoon, and finish crossing the flat in the cool of night.

Thank God for the moonlight.

It was dangerous enough crossing the desert in the day, but even more so at night. The horse could step in a hole, or worse, on a sidewinder, a tiger rattler, or even an Arizona coral.

He'd seen one colorful Mexican king snake, striped like a coral, during yesterday's ride, but had recited the old saying: Red to black a friend of Jack; red to yellow will kill a fellow. The king snake was nicely striped red and black. He'd just as soon not see "red to yellow."

He'd seen many a man become stingy with his water when faced with heat and sand, which could be a wise thing, but when you knew water was less than a half day away, you'd be better off carrying it in your belly than lugging it; or in your horse's belly if you wanted to ride rather than walk that half day.

But you had to be right.

Being wrong could be the last thing you ever did, besides feed the turkey vultures.

He rode until well after dark, finally seeing the lantern light flickering in the window of Dutchman's Station. They were across the flats and near the site of the Apache atrocity.

The only water was a sink directly behind the stage station, a stone's throw from the barn; half of the pool was fenced inside the station's stock corral.

Dismounting a quarter mile away, he studied the station. There was the faint sound of fiddle music. Someone was bowing a fiddle. He could see the outline of a wagon parked on the far side of the building, and could see it wasn't a heavy freight or express company Concord rig. Quietly, satisfied that they were busy inside, he led the dun and mule through scattered sage until he came upon a meadow. Even as hungry as the animals had to be, they ignored the grass and tugged Ryan forward to the water hole.

Ryan needed little encouragement, as the animals had watered hours after Ryan had drunk his last.

As the dun and mule drank deeply, Ryan fell on his belly and slowly sucked up as much water as he thought he could stand.

"I got water inside that's been standing and don't have the grit and mule piss in it," a voice called out.

Ryan rose. He'd left the Russian .45 hanging with a leather thong from the saddle horn.

"I didn't want to be a bother," Ryan said apprehensively.

"Ain't no bother. We got us a little shindig going on inside. You might as well join up."

The man stepped out of the moon shadow of the barn.

"I ain't much for shindigs," Ryan said, easing his way over to the dun and the Russian.

"That was obvious, or you'd'a yelled out at the house. But hell, man, you got to have been riding a long spell. You got a half-dollar? I got a bowl of venison stew inside . . . half a bucket worth, and hot coffee to boot, much as you can stomach."

As he spoke, the man moved closer. Ryan could see he wasn't armed.

When the man neared, he stuck out a long-fingered hand. He was as tall as Ryan, but thin as a wagon tongue, with a predominant Adam's apple that bobbed when he spoke.

"I'd be Matthew Andrews, and you're welcome to come on in for some cool, clean water and some fine fiddlin' even if you don't take supper."

Ryan shook with the man, liked the feel of his firm grip and the tone of his voice, and decided to risk it. He did not risk offering his name.

"You know," Ryan said, "I just happen to have four bits, even though that's the price of a fine beefsteak in most places . . . but a hot meal would sit well. I don't mind if I do."

"It's a long, hot ride to the nearest place to hunt deer. Ain't like we got a butcher around the next corner. You can sleep in a pile of soft hay in the barn, and for another

94

two bits, feed a hatful of grain . . . which I got to haul from the other side of Maricopa Flats . . . and a forkful of meadow hay to the horse and mule. I imagine they've earned it, pricey as it is."

"That they have, and I'll be happy to spend the two bits as well."

They stopped in the barn long enough for Ryan to pull off the chaps and beat his clothes out with the old felt hat, then stuff the .45 in his belt, unsaddle, rub down, grain, and stall the animals with a big forkful of hay. Only then did they head for the fiddle music.

The man held the door for Ryan, who entered with a little apprehension. He was surprised to see four men, one with a fiddle in hand, and one of them was Dr. Aaron Levy, his gray Vandyke beard and waxed mustache as perfect as always.

That pleased Ryan.

The man with the fiddle was black, and as Ryan looked closer, he realized that the third person wasn't a man at all, but a colored woman with her hair tied with a scarf. She rested a hand on the fiddler's thigh.

Another of the men, one equally Ryan's size, wearing a pair of revolvers butt-forward on his hips, sat back in his chair and his vest was parted.

He wore a tin star.

He rose, hands resting comfortably on the butts of stag-gripped matching Colts, and eyed Ryan thoughtfully.

That didn't please Ryan at all.

But he kept his face blank, and in fact managed a tight smile.

Eight

"I didn't catch your name," Andrews said.

"I didn't toss it out," Ryan said, replacing the tight smile with a wry but careful grin. "But it's Ronald . . . Ronald Overton," he said, the first name that came to mind.

Levy gave him a strange look, but went back to thoughtfully puffing on his pipe.

The introductions went round and Ryan nodded at the woman, removing his old beat-up hat, then shook with each man in turn, including Levy. Dr. Levy eyed him, shook, and nodded as if they'd never set eyes on each other.

The lawman was introduced as Ivan Metzler, a name Ryan recognized. He was a new territorial deputy marshal who had come to Phoenix during the time Ryan was standing trial in Prescott.

The lawman looked him up and down. "That blood on your trouser leg. You catch a cactus?"

"Nope, caught a bullet from a band of Indians thirty, forty miles back."

"The hell you say. Pimas?"

"I didn't pause to ask. I gave my mustang the spurs and didn't look back till it was too dark to ride."

"And the ear. They try to scalp you?" He smiled, appearently satisfied with the Indian tale.

"Nope, they tried to shoot my damn head off. My ear is still ringing."

The lawman laughed again, then asked, "What brings you to Dutchman's?"

Metzler retook his seat.

"Just traveling. On my way back to Illinois. Came out in sixty-five . . . to Montana."

That much was true.

"Panned enough color to get me to California, but I had enough of that after a dozen years." And that was partially true, but he'd come to Arizona after only five years in California.

"I'm goin' on home."

"You picked a hell of a time to travel, this heat and all," Metzler said, still eyeing him like a cat with a canary.

"I didn't know there was a good time in this miserable desert. An' I don't imagine you live hereabouts?"

"Humph," Andrews, the stationmaster, managed. Then he offered, "I come here with the consumption, but my lungs cleared up after two months of this dry air. I come to love the place . . . however, we need to clear the heathens out."

"You come by way of Yuma?" the deputy pressed Ryan.

"Just north of there a ways," Ryan lied with a straight face. "I followed the railroad, then cut over to the river the first I saw of it. Didn't call on the town. You headed there?" Ryan asked, trying to get the conversation off himself.

"I am, and dragging some trash."

He flicked his head to the side.

"Got two prisoners shackled around the side of the station . . . to a hitchin' rail."

He smiled, seemingly amused at the thought.

The hair rose on the back of Ryan's neck at the picture of two more men going to the hell that was Yuma Territorial Prison, but he said nothing, merely nodded.

Then he turned to Andrews. "You said you had a fine stew and some coffee?"

"Sorry. Hold on and I'll fetch it and throw in a pair of drop biscuits, if any's left. My Miriam makes the best biscuits in these parts."

"And a spoonful of honey, if you got it."

Ryan turned back to the seated men and woman.

"Don't let me stop the hoedown," Ryan said, knowing that the men wouldn't ask any more questions while the fiddle player worked.

In moments, Dr. Levy had left the room and returned from his wagon carrying his violin. He played three sad pieces, and not a word was spoken as he did; then he returned the instrument to his wagon.

Ryan ate to the accompaniment of the other instruments: the fiddle and a mouth harp played by the woman, who he presumed was the fiddler's wife.

He met Andrews at a table with benches near the door when the man returned, bowl and biscuits in hand.

Ryan said in a low voice, "I see the wire coming through here. You got a key?"

"I do, but the wire's down. Has been for most of a week. Damned Pimas or Apaches. . . ."

Ryan smiled.

He was due some good news.

Andrews gave him a strange look, but returned to the kitchen.

When finished with his supper — an excellent stew of venison, carrots, wild onions, and potatoes served by a rotund rosy-cheeked woman — he settled back as if content, and when the musicians put up their instruments, Ryan stood and yawned.

"You're right about the biscuits, Mr. Andrews. My compliments to the missus."

He stretched his arms wide and yawned again.

"Well, I'm up before the rooster, so I best find a soft spot in the hay."

"You going by way of Prescott?" the deputy asked.

"Could be," Ryan answered with a shrug.

"If you like fine vittles, try the Palace Hotel. They got an oyster sauce there that'll slick yer whistle."

Again, the hair rose on Ryan's neck. The Palace was one of many things owned by Leander Boyd, who, along with Nico Vaca, was on the top of his list of liars and cheats . . . men whom he was dedicated to shoot down like the dogs they were.

Instead of spitting on the floor, Ryan replied, "I knew someone who was going Prescott way. A lady. You know anyone in Prescott?"

"I should. I took the deputy's position there two years ago, after the other fella had some trouble."

It was all Ryan could do not to ask what kind of trouble, and see what lies had been told about him, but he continued his train of thought.

"A handsome woman, name of Felicia McCall," said Ryan.

"Handsome? Hell, man, she's one of the great beauties ever to bless the territory . . . a rose among thorns. How'd a drifter like you . . ."

Metzler reconsidered his words and eyed Ryan again with more than passing interest.

"How'd a fella comin' from California know a woman like that?"

Ryan lied with the expertise of a close-to-the-vest poker player.

"I shared a Concord coach with her some years ago in Colorado, at which time she said she was bound for Prescott, Arizona Territory. She's not a woman you'd soon forget." He smiled knowingly.

"That's for damn sure," the deputy said, ignoring the fact there was a woman in earshot.

Ryan could see the man's mind working, probably trying to remember how many years Felicia had been in Prescott, and if Ryan's story added up.

"She still there?" Ryan asked.

"On occasion. She's under the care and protection of one of the rich dons . . . Don

Nico Vaca. She comes into Prescott with him on rare occasions."

"Where does this Vaca hang his sombrero?" Ryan asked, wanting to confirm what he was sure he already knew.

"He's the emperor of his own domain. He's got four land grants, probably over a hundred thousand acres, but the one he frequents is Rancho Conejo, north of Phoenix and southeast of Prescott. To be more precise, south of the Mogollon Rim on Tonto Creek."

"Way out of my way," Ryan said with a shrug.

"It's not a place on which you'd make a casual call. His vaqueros, and there's a hundred or more of them, take a real dislike to anyone settin' foot on Vaca land. We've had to have a talk with the good don about his men ropin' and draggin' casual passersby. They hung a couple last year who helped themselves to one of his beeves.

"And he's got a foreman, Montez he's called. The meanest damn man ever to build a stairway to hell.

"Nope, I don't believe I'd just drop in, particularly not to have a visit with his woman . . . if'n that's what's going on up there."

The "his woman" grated Ryan's back-bone and he could feel the heat in his cheeks, but he collected himself.

"Then it'd be a good place to stay shy of, not that I'm heading that way nohow."

Ryan yawned again.

Aaron Levy rose from his chair. "I believe you and I are suite mates, mister . . . what did you say the name was?"

Ryan had to think a minute.

"Overton," he mumbled.

"I believe I'll walk you out, Mr. Overton, if you don't mind."

"Not at all, Doctor."

"I'll be along directly," the deputy said. "I'll be dragging those two outside into the barn as well. Don't let the rattling of chains be a bother."

Ryan gave him a hard look, but nodded.

The fiddle player also spoke up.

"We'll be in loft, if y'all don't mind. Our things is already there."

"More the merrier, I guess," Ryan said, wishing he'd passed on the stew and taken a spot under a mesquite instead, a mesquite far out in the desert.

In moments he and Dr. Levy had taken their leave.

As they walked to the barn, Levy cleared his throat.

104

"So, Mr. Overton," he asked with a slightly sarcastic tone, "you have some trouble back down the trail?"

Nine

Ryan stopped in his tracks and eyed the frail-appearing doctor with only a little apprehension.

"The name's O'Rourke, as you know, Doctor. Actually, it was a couple of the low-down dirty guards from the prison who had the trouble. Guards who damn nigh killed me a dozen times and stole my poke. The same fellas whose work you saw the result of when I was laid up at the Jenkins place."

"You were hurt bad. That sort of thing shouldn't happen to any man."

Levy stared off into the night for a moment, then turned back.

"So, you *damn nigh* killed them? An eye for an eye?"

"Nope, there wasn't no damn nigh about it. They're dead as of yesterday. But they drew down on me with my weapon still in my belt, and I had a roomful of witnesses, who may or may not have good eyesight."

"And it was the weapon I sold you . . . ?"

"It was."

Levy shook his head remorsefully. "Ah, a tool of the devil."

Ryan smiled tightly, with little enthusiasm. "A tool often used for God's work, often not, but a tool is only as good or bad as the craftsman. You can beat your swords into plowshares, Doctor, but then the other fella will still have a razor-sharp sword and be wantin' you to be at his beck and call."

Levy shook his head remorsefully. "And how does the law see this incident, Mr. Overton?"

"O'Rourke, as you know, but I appreciate your discretion. Who knows about the law, Dr. Levy . . . who knows? I do know that the law can be wrong as drought in December. Dead wrong at times. And when they are, it's often the other fellow, sometimes an innocent fella, who gets dead."

They entered the barn to the welcoming low nickering of the animals.

"So, how well will you sleep?" Levy asked, this time without sarcasm, but more as a party interested in the nature of man.

"Like a baby, Doctor. The sweet sleep of the redeemer. I should say the sleep of the

107

only partially redeemed. There will come a day, God willing, that I'll sleep soundly."

"I hope you do, my friend. However, hosanna should not be your cry when you've taken a life."

"I presume that's a little like a hooray?"

"A little."

"I'm not hooray'n, but I ain't losing no sleep neither."

Aaron Levy shrugged his shoulders. "There may be some men who need killing, it's not for me to say and I'll not presume to know God's will, about which it seems you're so sure . . . but I'm glad redemption, revenge really, is your task and not mine."

Ryan gave him a one-sided, halfhearted smile.

"Each of us to our own, Dr. Levy. Sleep well."

Levy nodded, then walked to the stall that held his mules. He nuzzled each of them on their soft muzzle, then, shaking his head sadly, found his way to his bedroll in a dark corner.

Ryan could hear Levy reciting his prayers as he fell into a sound sleep.

He awoke suddenly, the feel of cold steel shoved into his throat.

"Don't move, or I'll blow yer damn head off," a gruff voice commanded as he tried to focus his eyes.

It came to him with a start, even before he recognized the face.

Metzler, the deputy who'd taken his place in the Prescott marshal's office.

"Deputy," Ryan said. "What's the problem?"

"You're the problem, O'Rourke."

"Who's O'Rourke?" Ryan asked.

"You, that's who. I'm standin' up and movin' away. You jus' lie quiet. Don't you try to rise."

"Hell, I'm comfortable right here, now that you've taken that revolver outta my gullet."

Metzler stood upright, one stag-gripped Colt still trained on Ryan's head, the other holstered. He smiled. "I guess it's yer bad luck the wire's back up. Station-master got a message before the cock crowed this morning. You're wanted back in Yuma for shootin' down a couple of prison guards."

"The hell you say . . ." Ryan searched his mind for the name he'd used. "I'm Overton, not O'Rourke. You got the wrong man."

Metzler laughed. "Well, then you won't

mind riding back to Yuma with me and the boys . . . in chains, of course."

"I've never been in Yuma."

"It was the U.S. Army brand on the mule and the buttermilk dun gave you away, O'Rourke. That's a real unusual color for a horse. You should'a stole a sorrel."

"He bought that horse!" A voice rang out from the deep shadows.

Dr. Levy stepped out of the darkness where he'd been sleeping in an empty stall next to the mules.

His voice made the deputy snap his head around and divert the muzzle of the Colt. He'd gotten to his feet after awakening Ryan, but had not stepped quite far enough away.

Ryan hooked a toe behind his heel and kicked hard with the other foot to Metzler's knee.

The big deputy stumbled backward, allowing Ryan time to spring to a crouch with his feet under him and dive, catching the deputy at thigh level and knocking him the rest of the way to his back.

The Colt discharged with a roar that rocked the old barn, but over Ryan's head as they went down.

On his back, with Ryan astride him,

Metzler tried to bring his weapon back into play, but Ryan caught his wrist with one hand and delivered two smashing blows to the man's nose, then one to the jaw, with the free fist.

Metzler's eyes rolled up and he lolled his head back, blood spurting from a broken nose.

Ryan wrenched the Colt out of his hand, fished the other Colt out of its butt-forward holster, then stood, jumping back, not making Metzler's mistake, getting well out of both reach and kicking range.

"Please, sir, don't be shootin' up this way. They be innocent folk up here." The voice rang out from the loft. It was the fiddle player.

"Sorry," Ryan said. "You folks stay out of this and you'll have no trouble."

"We done had 'nuff trouble to last a lifetime, sir," the voice rang out again. "We be quiet as church mice."

"Shoot the sum'bitch," a voice rang out from the back of the barn.

"Yeah, shoot him."

It was the two prisoners Metzler had chained to a barn post.

"You two shut the hell up," Ryan said. "It'll be you gets shot if anyone does."

"This was not my intent," Levy said, stepping forward and kneeling at Metzler's side.

"He's not hurt . . . other than his pride," Ryan said.

"For not being hurt, he's blowing a devil of a lot of blood from his proboscis," Levy said, giving Ryan a disgusted look.

"His nose'll stop hurting a hell of a long time before I'd've gotten out of that hellhole, if I'd ever have gotten out, if I hadn't done what needed doing."

"Damn you, Levy," Metzler managed groggily.

"Damn me? Damn me, sir? I was just trying to right a wrong. This gentleman in fact did buy that horse. I was at the mine where he bought it."

Levy hadn't actually been there when Ryan bought the animal, but he knew the dun belonged to the Jenkins family, and was sure Ryan wouldn't steal from folks who'd offered him a helping hand.

"Then you knew he was O'Rourke?" Metzler accused.

"No, sir. Never did catch his name, and the mine was miles from Yuma. Owned by a fella name of Jenkins. Took me a while to realize this was the same man I'd seen there. He was bearded then; hairy as a Hasidic. Stay still while I pack your nostrils," Levy said.

He tore the pocket of Metzler's shirt away, and then tore it again into two pieces, which he wadded and stuffed into the deputy's nostrils to stem the bleeding.

"Leave those in as long as you can stand it. It'll help that nose heal straight."

Ryan sat on a log round and pulled on his boots as the nose-repair process went on. He searched for his Russian model, which had been in his bedroll.

"Where the hell is my weapon?" he snapped at Metzler just as the barn door swung aside.

It was just light enough that Andrews, the stationmaster, stood backlighted in the doorway. He was carrying a scattergun, holding it in both hands.

"Did you have to shoot him?" Andrews asked, thinking he was talking to Metzler, whom he'd informed about the killings and the buttermilk dun.

With one of Metzler's Colts in each hand, Ryan kept his voice steady.

"You lower that muzzle, friend, and I'll not have to blow you to hell. You and Mrs. Andrews treated me kindly. I'd hate to make her a widow woman."

"Mr. O'Rourke?" Andrews asked, but he

released the scattergun with one hand and used the free hand to shade his eyes, trying to focus into the dark barn. The muzzle swung upward, pointing at the sky.

"That would be me," Ryan said. "Nobody's shot here. At least not yet. I'll be taking my leave as soon as I saddle up. Mr. Metzler here will be riding my pack mule for a ways; then I'll send him back afoot.

"Don't any of you folks give us a follow, or I might mistake you for Apache and have to use that new Winchester of mine on them what is doggin' my trail."

"You're the law's business and the law's trouble," Andrews replied. "And I'm happy for it. I got a stage station to mind."

"Good. Then go to it. Leave the scattergun leaning against the door if you don't mind. It'll be there waiting for you after I'm gone."

"There's something else," Andrews said.

"What?"

"You got a wire, sent general delivery to all the stations along this line."

"Leave it lie there on the ground."

Andrews dropped the wire, then leaned the double-barrel on the doorway and disappeared.

Ryan had inspected the small feed and

tack room in the front corner of the barn and knew it was without a window, and he motioned the muzzle of the Colt at Metzler.

"Soon as you tell me where my revolver is, you can get yourself into that feed room and we'll sooner be on our way."

"I slung it over there in that pile of horse crap," Metzler said, his tone disgusted. "But that dun of yours will grow wings and fly before I go with you," he said adamantly.

"You're going, sitting in my packsaddle or out cold and throwed over it like a sack of road apples. It's your call. You'll be comin' back soon as I'm comfortable no one's a-doggin' me, and you'll have a good long walk."

"I'll die out there, afoot on Maricopa Flats."

"The more trouble you give me, the farther out there we'll be going afore I set you to walking. Keep yappin', and you just may feed your eyeballs to the buzzards."

"I can't leave these prisoners, so I couldn't be runnin' you down nohow."

"Says you. I say I'm gonna do it my way." Ryan moved a few steps and kicked through the stall rakings until he came up with the weapon. He wiped it on his pants, and still using one of the Colts, waved Metzler toward the tack room.

The man got to his feet, stomped over, and slammed the door behind him.

"Don't stick your head out lessen you want it blowed clean off," Ryan yelled after him, then picked up a pitchfork and walked over, buried the tines in the dirt, and jammed the handle into place, making a makeshift bar on the door.

Ryan jammed the Colt in his belt beside the Russian, then grabbed up his tack and headed for the corral adjoining the barn.

He motioned at Levy with his head to follow.

Levy helped him by saddling the pack mule. When they were done, after leading the animals back to the barn door, Ryan paused a minute while he picked up the paper Andrews had dropped. He didn't waste time reading it, rather stuffed it into his shirt pocket. Then he laid a hand on the doctor's shoulder.

"I appreciate all you've done, Doctor."

"It was not my intent to interfere with the law, Ryan. You should know that. I try to live my life abiding the laws of God and man . . . in that order, of course."

"Nonetheless, you've been a help, and I won't forget it."

As they entered the barn, Metzler began banging hard on the inside of the door, trying to knock the pitchfork aside.

Ryan pulled the Smith and Wesson and aimed at the door.

"No!" Levy shouted, but the roar of the .45 reverberated through the barn.

"He shot him, he shot him," rang an exuberant cry from the prisoners chained out of sight in the back of the barn.

"Damn your hide!" the voice growled from inside the room. Ryan had blown a hole in the plank wall well above the door.

"You settle down in there," Ryan commanded, then hoisted the panniers in place and filled them with his sacks of goods.

"Jehovah!" Levy sighed, his voice weak. "I thought you might have shot him."

"I normally don't shoot folks for trying to do their job," Ryan said, swinging up in the saddle. "However, I might make an exception in Metzler's case. Kick that fork out of there, please," he asked Levy, who walked over, applied his brogan, and sent the pitchfork flying.

Metzler appeared in the doorway, hands on hips, eyeing the .45 trained on his belly.

"You gonna shoot me down like a cur dog?" he asked Ryan.

"Metzler, comparing yourself to a dog is

117

an insult to canines. Climb up in that packsaddle and lead the way east."

"I told you, I ain't . . ."

Ryan dropped the muzzle a few inches and blew barn dirt out from between Metzler's legs. The roar of the shot reverberated through the barn as the dust settled.

"Damn," Metzler yelled, paling, as dust motes floated down from the loft above.

"Please, y'all don't be shootin' up here," the fiddler's voice rang out again.

"In the saddle, Deputy," Ryan commanded.

Metzler hurried over and tried to mount the packsaddle, but the lack of stirrups and the bags in his way didn't allow it.

"Dr. Levy," Ryan requested, and Levy stepped over and made a cradle of his hands, boosting Metzler up.

"Doctor, if you'd do us one more favor. Go back to Metzler's outfit and fetch him a canteen of water. He'll likely be needing it."

Levy did so, and handed it up to the deputy.

"Lead out," Ryan commanded.

"You gonna steal my Colts?" Metzler accused. "My daddy gave me those when I become a deputy."

"He's no *gonnif*," Levy said.
"What?" Metzler asked.
"Just ride," Ryan commanded.

Ten

It was dreadfully hot by mid-morning. The sparse grass did little to keep the sun from reflecting off the white alkali plain. In the distance, false lakes shimmered.

When he figured they'd traveled five or six miles, Ryan yelled up to Metzler, who was plugging ahead, his head hanging. "Deputy, rein up."

The man did so with the single lead rope and the obedient mule stopped, hanging his head to nibble at a handful of stiff grass.

Ryan studied his back trail.

No sign of pursuers; no telltale dust of hard-riding men.

"Climb down, and take that canteen of water with you."

The big man did so, but didn't start away. He merely stood, staring, his eyes filled with fire.

"You sum'bitch, I'll get you for this."

"Save your breath, Deputy. You'll need it for the stroll back."

"I'll die out here, and you'll hang. Hell, you're gonna hang anyhows."

"You may die, but if you do it'll be from stupidity . . . which makes me more than a mite concerned about the likelihood that you'll die."

"And if the savages come along?"

"I'm going to ride another three hundred yards and then I'm dropping these Colts in the dirt. You don't take a step that way until you see them fall. There's track as clear as springwater all the way back to the station. Even a dullard like you should be able to follow it. Now drop the lead rope and move away from the mule."

He did so and Ryan moved up, gathering up the mule and spurring the dun on east.

After a few hundred yards, he dropped the Colts as promised, hearing shouts well behind him.

"I'll get you, you sum'bitch! I'll get you!"

Ryan couldn't help but smile, but he hurried the dun for a couple of hundred yards. He'd be a quarter mile away by the time the deputy got to his firearms, and if Metzler was smart, he'd save what shells he had.

Ryan had always figured that wearing two guns was nothing but show. If you

121

couldn't get the job done with one, it wasn't likely the other would do much good. And they were heavy on the hip. He figured that by the time Metzler got back to the stage station, he'd feel the same way.

Satisfied he'd left the man in good stead — angry and resentful, but alive and spittin' — he moved on. He had fifteen hard miles to go; then the country would ease a little.

He stayed well north of the stage road, but south of the dry bed of the Gila River, which had turned away almost due north. At one time he reined up to rest the animals and watch the stage in the distance, a mile or more away, as it rolled by. Here, across this arid plain, the stage company used mules, as they were tougher and the lack of water didn't deplete them as it did horses.

It was almost dark when he saw the Maricopa Wells Stage Station in the distance.

A quarter mile from it, a small village of Pima Indians resided in a permanent camp of mud-and-willow-branch huts. He stayed well north of both, knowing, if the old sergeant's information was correct, that he'd find a seep of water surrounded by willows.

He did, precisely as the old man had described, having to avoid an Indian melon and squash patch nearby, which was irrigated by the seep, but it was untended and drying in the sun with only the remnants of a crop left.

He hobbled the animals and let them graze in sparse grass surrounding the seep, and made a cold camp under a single cottonwood tree, not willing to risk a fire, sure that the wire was humming with the news from Yuma, and the fact the shooter was heading east.

Finding two melons that were beginning to wither but inside were still sweet and moist, he had them to supplement his dinner of jerky and dry biscuits.

In the morning, he'd have to make a decision: Follow the stage road to Tucson, or head north, skirting the White Tank Mountains and picking up the Fria River.

Not long after that it would be decision time again: northwest up the Cottonwood Valley to Prescott and Captain Leander Boyd, Filo Parkinson, and Henry Holstadt, all jury members who'd intimidated the others until they found him guilty; or northeast across the New River Mountains to Tonto Creek and up it to Rancho Conejo, Nico Vaca, and very likely, Felicia McCall.

He knew the answer. Like the fools most men were, he'd follow his heart and the heat in his loins.

As he unrolled his bedroll, he remembered the telegram Andrews had received and passed along.

He reclined in the fading light, fished it out of his pocket, and read.

R. O'Rourke.
Just heard you're released. A hundred-dollar draft is waiting for you at the Miners and Merchants Bank in Phoenix. What else can we do?

Kin

Ryan smiled. It was only the second time he'd heard from most of his kinfolk since he'd gone to prison. The first time was merely signed as this one was, "Kin," and it asked him if he'd like to be like a redtail hawk, and he knew exactly what it meant: Would he like them to break him out of Yuma Prison? He'd replied he'd rather be like a clam, and could lie in the sand for a couple of years, and that they'd hear from him if he changed his mind.

He'd almost weakened several times and written them, but he'd stayed strong, not wanting to risk his "kin." His sister, Kathleen, a successful actress, and one of

124

only two females of his generation, wrote him several letters, only one of which he answered.

Early on, when Kathleen was but sixteen and her talent was recognized, the whole family had pitched in to send Kathleen to St. Louis, then to New York, then to Paris to refine her singing and acting, supporting her for ten years. She'd paid them back twice.

His cousins, Ethan and Dillon McCabe, were cattle ranchers in Montana; and neither they nor his other cousins, Reese, Garret, and Clair Conner, were given to writing, although Garret should have been, as a former teacher of literature aspiring at one time to become a professor. Garret and his brother Reese were as different as summer and winter. Reese operated just on the edge of the law, a gambler and gunfighter, should he feel the cause just. Reese had been a lawman for a short time. Not that the professor couldn't handle a gun; he damn well could, far better than most men, having been a sniper in the service of the Confederacy.

But all of them were family — kin — and kin meant more than just a little something to all of them.

It was life and death, if it came to that.

The fact was when they were all young, way too young to take advantage of their grandfather's fine sour mash whiskey, they'd taken a blood oath: Wrong one of the kin, and you'd wronged them all.

He had no idea which of them had sent the telegram and wired the draft, because each of them knew they could speak for the others when it came to helping kin.

Ryan could use the hundred dollars.

The question was, could he risk walking into the Miners and Merchants in Phoenix? He decided he'd cross that bridge when faced by its planks in front of him.

One thing he knew for sure. This was his problem and his alone and he could handle it.

He wouldn't risk dragging kin into it.

They had their own lives now, and didn't need the kind of hornet's nest he was about to stir.

The night had cooled to tolerable sleeping temperature and the stars were his blanket. The horse and mule were hobbled and enjoying the remnants of the melon and squash patch. He'd made it across the worst of Maricopa Flats . . . and he'd make it the rest of the way.

He checked the wound on his leg and found it healing nicely. He redressed it, satisfied that he would die from something else.

His was a quest, and he wouldn't be denied.

An owl's lonely lament coaxed him to sleep.

"I told you, *querida*" — Nico referred to her with the endearing term "darling" — "that I forbid you to ride alone. Even though a mare, your little Andalusian is very spirited. I would want nothing . . ." She did not answer, and his anger quieted.

She'd been leaving the grounds, riding into the desert without escort. Even though the Rancho Conejo settlement was a veritable fortress, the rancho lands were large and dangerous, for the Apache still reigned in many of the distant canyons and arroyos. And no one knew when they might appear to steal horses, or women.

He walked to the shutters and stood staring out over his domain, a small *azote,* a quirt, in hand, slapping it softly on the side of his leg.

She had not responded to his touch, nor accompanied him to his quarters since, they'd had the conversation regarding Señor O'Rourke. He seethed in quiet anger, but knew that anger was not the way to get what he wanted . . . what he needed . . . from this hot, high-strung woman.

He spun back to face her where she sat, primly, book in hand, reclined in a hide-covered, horsehair-stuffed chair.

"Are you listening to me?"

"I hear you just fine, Nico."

He stomped over and stood looking down at her.

"So, have you thought of your old friend Ryan O'Rourke?"

She cut her eyes upward. "What of him?"

"He's a murderer and a coward," Nico said, fishing a paper out of his pocket. "He shot to death two unarmed men . . . guards from the prison that has been his home for the last two years. Unarmed men, who were merely enjoying themselves in a local cantina. He's now a wanted man, after only a few days being free."

He threw the message down in her lap, then spun on his heel, his voice raised as he stomped from the room.

"This is the kind of man who you have for a friend. A murderer, a coward."

He stopped at the door leading out of the great room and turned back to her.

"If you insist on riding away from the

hacienda alone, I will ban you from the *establo*. . . . I will tell Montez you are not to ride."

"If you do, Señor, I will find my own way back to Prescott."

"A threat, *querida?*"

His eyes sparked as he glared at her. "You threaten me, your savior, your protector. I think not. It's a very long walk to Prescott, little one. A very, very long walk."

He turned and walked out of the room, yelling back, slapping the quirt on his leg as he did so.

"You too can be tamed, little one, just as I tamed the mare I gave you."

The heavy front door to the hacienda slammed with a resounding crash that echoed throughout the building.

A part of the message had been torn away at a fold, leaving only the words:

. . . hanging him. Wires have been sent to all stations and towns in the territory. O'Rourke will hang, or be shot by some ambitious soul, long before he can possibly become a problem for us.

Lee Boyd

She wondered how the rest of the message read. There was nothing here to indicate that Ryan had shot unarmed men, and she knew better.

If anything, Ryan O'Rourke was much too bold, much too willing to confront those who wanted to do him or his harm. And he was a fair man, sometimes far too fair for his own good. She had once enticed Ryan into her bed, telling him she feared and hated her betrothed, Sam Polkinghorn. Ryan had seemed a simple man, but a man of some means, and a good backup should her relationship with Sam have gone awry. And it did, to her surprise, with Ryan O'Rourke shooting Sam Polkinghorn dead. By that time, she'd met Nico Vaca, the richest man in Arizona Territory.

She smiled quietly, wondering what Nico had done with the rest of the message, and what it said.

She made up her mind to find it, even if she had to return to Nico's room to do so.

Nico stomped into the *establo* and yelled for Montez.

His *segundo* had been with him for many years. Nico had saved him from a Mexican prison, spiriting him out of Mexico to the Arizona ranch after Montez, as a hot-blooded young vaquero, had killed

130

two men in a cantina for a slur against Nico, his *jefe*. Since that time, Montez had risen quickly as a trusted employee of Vaca's, serving not only as a vaquero, and finally as *segundo,* but in the much more important role of protector of all things Vaca.

He was quick with a reata, knife, or *pistola*. A skilled *pistolero* who by now had killed more men than Nico cared to remember, but always in defense of things Vaca, of Rancho Conejo, and the other ranchos.

But they had to be careful of letting him go below the border, as he was still wanted there by the *soldados*. It seemed one of the men he killed in the cantina was the nephew of the governor.

He was a hard man, and Nico's favorite among many. Finally, he walked into the barn, stretching and yawning.

"*Sí, jefe,* you called?"

"I did, *hijo.*" Even though there was only fifteen years' difference in their ages, Nico thought of him as a son.

"I wish to sit and drink some *pulque* and talk of Señor O'Rourke."

Montez eyed him carefully. "O'Rourke, the man I took to the mountains, the man who slew the largest elk of that season?"

"Yes, that man. He is coming, and this time, it is he who will feel hot lead in his liver."

Ryan awoke, light just painting the eastern sky, to the sound of low voices, guttural mumbling that he didn't recognize — but there was no one in sight.

He'd slept with his saddle as a pillow and the Russian at his side and the Winchester in the scabbard in easy reach, and he palmed the revolver quickly and quietly in his right hand and held the rifle in his left.

In moments he'd pulled on his boots and, crouching, made his way to where he thought the sound originated, the melon and squash patch.

He rose to full height, revolver leveled, rifle hanging casually, to see a pair of Indians in loincloths, bodies decorated in black stripes, faces painted coal-black, lips painted red, removing the hobbles from the buttermilk dun.

Eleven

Pimas, from the nearby village; one carried a bow, the other an ancient single-shot cap-and-ball, but it lay in the withered-vine-covered dirt beside him.

They already had a lead rope on the mule and his hobbles off.

Busy, they still hadn't noticed him, until he spoke up just as they got the hobbles off the dun.

"Hey, what the hell do you think you're doing?"

They spun and rose in the same instant, bow and rifle in hand, staring at him, eyes wide. The one with the old cap-and-ball started to bring the muzzle up.

Ryan cocked the Russian and centered it on the brave's chest, shaking his head no, but the rifle kept coming. Almost guiltily, he dropped the muzzle and fired, taking the man in his thick thigh and blowing his leg out from under him.

As his friend went down, the second brave broke and ran, stumbling in the vines until he cleared them, then sprinting like a mustang that's scented a mare on the wind.

Ryan moved over and kicked the old muzzle-loader away, then kneeled by the man who had yet to cry out, but was obviously in great pain. The bullet had passed through his leg cleanly, but very close to the bone. It could be broken, but Ryan doubted it.

Kicking the muzzle-loader ahead of him, he moved back to his camp and dug out and cut away a couple of pieces of tent cloth and returned and knelt down, tore one in half, packed the wound front and back, then bound it tightly, hoping that would stop the flow of blood.

He shook his head in disgust, then rose and returned to his camp, leading the mule and dun.

In moments, he was packed and on his way. Those at the stage station would have heard the shot and might come to investigate, and the Indian he let flee might return with a dozen more.

Hell, he wasn't yet into true Apache country, and he'd already had Indian trouble.

The country was beginning to rise in elevation, and the starkness of Maricopa Flats began to be replaced with rock out-croppings, cactus, and a few scattered saguaros. Some of them rose to thirty feet, lording it over all other desert vegetation.

He struck out due north, knowing that in a day or a little more he'd cross the Maricopa Mountains, then come to the Salt River. Upstream along it for a few miles should, a day later, bring him to Phoenix, and then he'd have to make up his mind about the hundred dollars that awaited him.

Of course, every lawman in the territory knew the hundred dollars awaited him, as they would all have been made privy to the wire he'd received from the kin.

He traveled only a half day, constantly checking his back trail, until he stumbled on a grove of narrow-leaf cottonwood lining a small creek that rose up out of the ground and only traveled a half mile before it disappeared again into the sand.

It was not only the trees and fresh water that convinced him to stop, but the temperature. It was at least ten to fifteen degrees hotter than the day before, well over a hundred degrees, but not hot enough that the big antelope jackrabbit that jumped out of a patch of cactus didn't run almost a hundred yards before stopping.

That had been the rabbit's last mistake, as the dun was more than happy to stand dead still, and the Winchester was dead on.

He skinned the rabbit and hung him up while he stripped away a roasting stick, then a pile of bark from the cottonwoods, shredded the bark with his knife, knowing that the mule and probably the horse would feed on it after they grazed off what little grass the banks of the trickle offered. It left a lot to be desired as fodder, but it was filling.

The fresh-roasted meat was welcome, but having made a fire had him worried, so he left the horse and mule hobbled, his bedroll laid out and stuffed with his goods as if a heavy man rested there, and moved away to the shade of a rock shelf sheltered from view by a hedge of cholla cactus, where he reclined and tried to sleep the day away. He was entertained for a while by a whip snake, trying his best to climb the cholla to reach a white-wing dove's nest.

The snake finally gave up, as did Ryan. His full belly and a slight breeze helped him surrender to exhaustion, and soon he was sleeping soundly.

Ryan was getting near civilization and,

with the heat and that fact, he'd decided it was time to travel at night.

Awaking just at dusk, he moved down toward the camp, peering over a low line of prickly pear, studying the camp and the peaceful horse and mule.

Their heads hung, seemingly undisturbed by anything. The pile of shredded cottonwood bark was half-gone. As there was no sign of anything out of order, he hurried down, repacked, and just as a nearly full moon climbed over the mountains to the east, gave the dun his head and they were moving north at a steady pace; north to Phoenix, then north by northeast to Rancho Conejo, and Felicia.

He'd thought it through on the long ride.

Nico Vaca was the worst of the lot, and if Ryan was successful in shooting down that dog, maybe he'd let the others stew in their own juices, worrying about when he was coming. He'd see if there was a future for him and the girl, then let her weigh into his decision regarding Lee Boyd, Filo Parkinson, and Henry Holstadt.

Parkinson and Holstadt had merely been flunkies, doing what they were told, and that should weigh somewhat into what he did to them.

Theirs was a sin of omission — not bothering to tell the truth. Maybe he'd merely shoot their ears off? Then again, his own ear was notched and that hadn't slowed him much.

Lee Boyd was another matter. He was the main organizer of the vigilante committee, along with Vaca, and the main reason that Ryan had been falsely imprisoned.

Theirs were sins of commission — it was their crime he'd confronted in the first place, and they'd set the jury up and threatened those on the jury they didn't own.

Lee Boyd and Nico Vaca had to pay dearly.

He didn't stop until midday, on the sinks of the Salt, where he knew he'd find brackish but drinkable water in sinkholes and some graze.

They were only a couple of miles from the old town of Phoenix, but he had no desire to enter the village in daylight.

He waited in the wispy shade of a pair of spiny catclaw trees until the sun touched the rim of the Maricopas to the west.

He made a picket line between the two catclaw trees, where the horse had some shade, could reach water and what little graze there was.

He found a cache to hide his goods in a thick prickly pear stand, then saddled his mule.

The buttermilk dun had given him away one time, and he didn't want there to be a second. The mule took well to the saddle although he took some umbrage at the spoon bit, and by the time it was dark he was clomping into the center of town.

Most of Phoenix was adobe, but clap-board and ripped-wood-plank buildings, and even a couple of cut-stone two-story ones — the Miners and Merchants Bank being one of them — signified the center of the growing territorial town.

He passed on through and stopped a block past the bank where a sign said TOWBRIDGE'S, the first saloon to the north of the bank.

The batwing doors were tied open, and the music of a piano wafted out into the street. Lugging the Winchester, the Russian stuffed into his belt, he made his way through low-hanging cigar smoke to the only vacant spot at the busy, well-polished bar, put his foot up on a brass foot rail, and slapped the polished wood for the bartender's attention just as if he cared little who noticed him.

The bartender gave him a nod and finished pulling a couple of beers, then moved down the bar.

"What's yer pleasure?"

"Beer, cold and running over."

"How about cool and filled to the brim? There ain't nothing cold, other than my old lady's heart, within five hundred miles."

Ryan nodded, then turned to eye the place as the man said, "Bowl of goobers is only a nickel."

The floor was covered with peanut shells.

"No, thanks."

The bartender shrugged and went to draw the beer.

Two tables offering faro were full of players, and a third table held five men playing poker.

Ryan got his beer, flipped a dime to the bartender, took a deep draw, then used one of the towels hanging at four-foot intervals to wipe the foam out of his several days of whisker growth.

He crossed the room to lean against the wall and watch the poker game. Three of the men looked to be drovers or freighters, and the other two city men, both in waistcoats even in the heat, wearing watch fobs and chains securing engraved gold watches.

"We got a chair here, mister, you got a five-dollar gold piece?" one of the players suggested.

"I believe I'll watch a while and get the feel of the game," Ryan said with a nod.

It was an average game with probably not more than fifty dollars between the players; and a friendly one, as they chatted about the Apache troubles, mining, and city business, until one question caught Ryan's interest.

"Horace, how's my money doing?" one of the other players asked.

He was one of the city fellows, who looked as if he hadn't seen hard work since he was weaned. He was almost as big around as the table, with pig eyes and hog jowls.

Just as Ryan centered his eyes on the speaker, a bar girl in a low-cut kelly-green gown sidled up beside him.

"Hey, big fella, buy a girl a drink?"

"No, ma'am," Ryan said, ignoring her.

"You ain't in no shantytown, big man. Your manners stink like the south end of a northbound skunk," she said, losing most of the phony smile.

Ryan shrugged his shoulders and gave her a hard look until she stomped off.

After being two years in the company of

smelly men, it wasn't the easiest thing he'd ever done, shooing her away.

Luckily, his confrontation with the girl had distracted the players.

Finally, after studying his cards, the other man in city clothes held his cards close and laughed before he finally answered the first city fellow.

"Why don't you come visit it, Tiny? It's just laying there earning you more money. And when you do, bring me another pile to lend out."

"Maybe I'll do that. In fact, maybe I'll take out a loan so I can expand the hotel."

"Sure, Tiny. I'd love to loan you your own money back and charge you a couple of percent more than I'm paying you for the deposits."

Now it was Tiny's turn to laugh.

"I just bet you would, Horace." He laid down his cards, three queens, and smiled broadly, revealing a gold front tooth.

"Hell, I believe I'd rather win it from you than borrow it," said Tiny. "It's a hell of a lot cheaper."

The fat man guffawed and reached for the pot.

"Not so cheap as you think," Horace, who was obviously the town's banker, said with a wide grin, laying down an ace-high spade flush.

"You highbinder," the big man said, but smiling.

But he wasn't smiling so much as Ryan was. This could be the answer to his dilemma.

He walked back to the bar and splurged on his second beer, leaning the rifle against the bar as he enjoyed it.

As soon as he was done, he gathered up the rifle and headed out.

Untying the mule, he led him back toward the bank building, then again tied him, but this time directly across the side street from the granite building; then he returned toward the saloon. He took a seat in front of a tonsorial parlor, under a red-and-white-striped pole, two buildings down, between the saloon and bank.

Making himself as comfortable as the hard bench would allow, he watched the comings and goings at the saloon for well over an hour, until the man he'd presumed was the banker walked out, luckily alone, and now wearing a top hat and carrying a walking stick. He headed back up the street, a path that would take him directly in front of where Ryan rested.

Ryan feigned sleeping, lolling his head

back against the clapboard, until the man that had been called Horace drew even with him.

He let him pass a couple of steps, then called out, "Horace."

The man stopped and turned.

"Do I know you, sir?"

"No, sir, I don't believe I've had the pleasure." Ryan rose and extended a hand. They shook, but the man was not particularly pleased or impressed by the encounter.

"You are familiar, sir."

"You mean my look or my manner?"

"Your manner, sir. I'm Horace Tobias Renforth the Third, and it would be proper for you to address me as Mr. Renforth."

Ryan smiled, as he slipped the Russian out of his belt.

"You're right, Mr. Renforth; however, I was not privy to your last name."

Renforth paled, and began to bring the walking stick up.

Ryan cocked the Russian. "I'd hate to have to shoot you, Mr. Renforth. I don't know you well enough to blow you all to hell . . . at least not yet. Killing a fella is a mite on the familiar side."

Twelve

The man lowered the walking stick.

Ryan smiled as the banker blanched.

"I've seen that particular model walking stick before. Thirty-two caliber, if memory serves me."

"It also serves well as a pointer, sir."

"It should, as it has a concealed blade as well. So, as it's such a fine pointer, Mr. Renforth, point it at the bank. We've got some business."

Renforth puffed up like a desert horned toad about to spit blood, and stammered, "I . . . I only know one half the combination to the vault, so it'll do you . . . do you no good until my cashier arrives in the morning. My cashier takes his morning coffee with the territorial marshal, and he usually accompanies Wilfred to the bank. . . . So if I were you, I'd hightail it out of town right now."

"You mean territorial *deputy* marshal. The marshal hangs his hat in Prescott. I said business, not thieving, Mr. Renforth.

145

Now move along before I take offense at you trying to use that toy on me, and me just trying to do a little legitimate transaction."

"Humph," Renforth managed, but he turned and started up the street, just as the boisterous voices of men leaving the saloon echoed behind him.

The banker started to pause and turn, but Ryan shoved the Russian into his back, compelling him to keep moving.

"You'll never get away —"

"I told you, this is business. I admit my methods are a bit unorthodox, but business nonetheless."

"Humph," the banker managed again.

In moments, after Renforth removed a heavy padlock from the thick front doors, they were inside the bank. Renforth reached into his waistcoat pocket and brought out a lucifer to light a lamp, but Ryan called him off.

"Don't do it. There's light enough for what little business we have."

He dug into his shirt pocket and came out with the wire.

"I received this back down the trail a ways. Seems you have a hundred-dollar draft drawn on the telegraph company, payable to Ryan O'Rourke, who would be me. I'd like to have it, in gold, please."

The banker was quiet for a moment.

Then he said, his tone supercilious, "Come back in the morning, Mr. O'Rourke, and we'll conclude this then. I don't do business —"

"Yes, sir, you do. Make out a receipt and I'll sign it, soon as you give me one hundred in gold."

Again the man let out a hard breath, but he shoved through a little swinging gate made of turned posts and went to a wide desk. He sat and reached for a drawer to open it.

"Stop right there. I'll get you a pen and paper. I presume your inkwell is full?"

Ryan rounded the desk and opened the drawer Renforth had reached for. A shiny nickeled revolver lay on top of a couple of ledger books.

"Mr. Renforth, that was downright unsociable. Now fish out a foolscap and get to writing your receipt, so I can get on my way. There's a pretty little señorita in Tucson pining away for me."

Ryan had let the hammer down on the Russian, but now, when the banker didn't move, he cocked it again. The banker quickly fished a piece of notepaper out of another drawer and scribbled out a receipt, blotted it, then handed it over. Ryan grabbed the pen and scratched his name as the banker turned his oak chair, bent, and went to work on the combination to a small green, gold-trimmed safe in a cabinet behind his desk.

"I don't suppose there's another little troublemaker in the safe?" Ryan asked, pressing the muzzle of the Russian behind the banker's ear.

"That's a foolhardy thing to do, Mr. Ryan. That weapon's cocked."

"Not as foolhardy as you trying to pull another weapon, Renforth. Hell, you'd think I was robbin' the place."

In moments, Ryan had five shiny twenty-dollar gold pieces in hand.

"I'll leave this little pistol at the front door," Ryan said.

Still carrying the Winchester in hand, he shook it at the man.

"I'm sure you have a little work to do. Don't stick your head out the front door for fifteen minutes or so, or I'll have to try and hole that top hat of yours, and I might miss . . . even as accurate as this Winchester seems to be. It's been a pleasure doing business with you, Mr. Renforth. I'd tip my hat, but it seems my hands are full."

Ryan backed out of the door, spun on his heel, and walked quickly across the side street to the mule, mounted, and rode north out of the little town, then circled and headed back to where he'd left the dun.

Leading the mule at a canter, he was soon headed east in the rocky Salt River bottom, figuring he'd move a couple of miles that way before he turned back north.

The moon was now directly overhead, and he had plenty of light, but even at that, he slowed the animals to a single-foot, as he wouldn't risk the dun stepping into a hole.

It had all gone way too easy.

It was noon, the sun high above him and burning down, when he saw the dust rising behind him. He'd been pulling up continually, following game trails through mesquite thickets, winding but working his way north, always north, when he'd paused on a rise to check his back trail.

He watched for a long moment, convincing himself that what he was seeing was the result of dying dust devils, but no, it was the rising dust of riders.

Several riders.

Who, other than a posse, would be crazy enough to ride at that pace in this killing heat?

He'd chased enough men on the trail to

know that he had the advantage. Whoever it was had had to find his trail, then ride like hell to catch up. He knew they hadn't been on the trail in the darkness, as the country he'd been crossing was hardpan, broken by patches of mesquite and prickly pear and hard to track in even in full light — which meant they'd had to leave at first light, only five or six hours ago.

No, they'd ridden hard, and were riding spent animals. He should have no trouble outdistancing them.

There was a rock ridge only a half mile or so ahead, where he could climb to get a good look at his back trail, where he could look down into the tall mesquite and have a chance of counting his pursurers.

Gigging the dun, he moved forward at an easy trot until he reached the bottom of an escarpment that rose to tall spires. He dropped rein and lead rope in a patch of grass, and leapt from the saddle and scrambled up the broken shale until he had sixty or seventy feet on the animals, but still he could only intermittently see riders move in and out of the mesquite, maybe three-quarters of a mile behind.

He moved higher, until he reached the base of almost vertical rock, then hunkered down in the shade of an overhang.

Making eight or nine riders, moving at a canter, he watched for only a moment.

The two men in front rode paint horses, and sat easy on horseback. Indian scouts, Pimas or Maricopas, he figured.

The four men in the rear were leading horses.

That bothered Ryan somewhat.

Men who planned to ride down one horse and mount another seemed a bit determined.

The Indians would know the country, and they'd be hard to shake. One of the others was probably the deputy marshal in Phoenix, a man known well to Ryan: James "Jeeter" McCoy, a hard man but one with little ambition to whom Ryan had never gotten close. The rest were more than likely drovers or townsmen out on an adventure. The first time a .44/40 from the Winchester buzzed over their heads, they'd be wondering why they weren't back in the saloon.

Jeeter too would look for every opportunity to head home . . . depending upon how much money was on Ryan's head, if any. He had the worst arrest record among any of the marshals.

And the Indian scouts would have little interest in Ryan, unless the money was good enough to buy them a month's worth of Who Hit John and a few trips to the hay with a cantina girl.

He slipped and slid back to the horse and mule, took the time to give them each a hat full of water, took a mouthful himself, mounted, then headed north around the razor-back ridge where he couldn't be easily sighted.

It was time to pound ground.

He set an easy canter, still moving uphill, seeing a ridge top, not much more than a low swell ahead. When he crossed it, if it was downhill for a ways and good even ground, and with enough holes in the mesquite thickets, he could put the animals into a gallop for a while. They couldn't keep up that pace for long in this heat, but neither could his pursuers.

Felicia McCall had been on her own for more than twenty years, and a woman in the West couldn't accomplish that without being somewhat of a business person; a negotiator of some merit.

Last night, wanting to find the rest of the note Nico had shown her, she went to his room. When she appeared, he was in his nightshirt, standing at the shutters, smoking a cigarillo, staring out over his expansive rancho.

He gave her a knowing smile when she appeared in his doorway, after a demure knock.

He waved her in, walked over, and encircled her waist with a thin but strong arm, bent, and tried to kiss her. She met the attempt with a hand separating their lips.

After a long conversation regarding what she meant to him, and how much she was valued, and after his agreeing to let her accompany him to Prescott, she returned the kiss.

The following morning, she cooed as he arose, telling him she needed her beauty sleep and her rest if she was going to spend a week or more in the demanding nightlife of Prescott, and he dressed and left her to luxuriate in his big bed.

He wasn't gone more than fifteen minutes when she went to the shutters, opened them a crack, and spied on him and his *segundo,* Montez, standing outside the *establo* doors, drinking coffee and discussing the day's work.

She hated and feared Montez.

He was a tall man with a hawk nose who looked at her as if she were a piece of meat in his talons. She'd never seen him smile, but had seen him mistreat many a horse and the other vaqueros on the rancho. One time he'd whipped a stable boy, marking him badly, for not properly saddling the big black stallion he almost always rode. And she'd seen him viciously spur a young horse whom he thought to make one of his string, until the animal had intestines bulging from the cuts in the side of his belly. The animal had had to be put down.

Yes, Montez was a man to whom she would barely speak. But Nico found him to his liking, so she had to tolerate him.

It took her another fifteen minutes to find the rest of the note, amongst other papers in his rolltop desk in a sitting room next to his bedroom.

She was not surprised to read:

O'Rourke worked at a mine outside of Yuma for a month. He returned and confronted head prison guard Ike McGillicutty, and guards Shott and Parsons, in a Yuma cantina. He goaded them into drawing on him and killed the head guard and one other. The warden there said he might be able to make a case, given time, but it's up to a bunch of local roughnecks who are all that's available to serve, and it seems the guards are not well thought of by the locals.

It was a fair fight, but he's wanted for a hearing.

He bought a light-colored dun and a mule with an army brand. I've posted a five-hundred-dollar reward for his capture and sent wires and had some posters printed.

You will pay *one half this fee.*

I did not mention *in the poster that he was only wanted for questioning and to testify at a hearing. With luck, some overzealous bounty hunter will bring him in dead, due to my unfortunate omission, and save us the trouble of* —

And it was torn there. She remembered the portion of the note Nico had shown her, which began with "hanging him."

It had been signed by Lee Boyd, Nico's partner in many ventures in Prescott.

It was just like Boyd and Nico to try to use the law to do their dirty work. They'd used it before on Ryan O'Rourke, and other men, and would again if they could. Owning most of the law was a definite advantage.

The portion of the note Nico had shown her certainly had not mentioned that Ryan had killed two of them in a fair fight, when he was outnumbered.

155

It was as she'd guessed.

He'd probably had very good reason, if he was still the man she remembered.

She wondered, would he return to Prescott? And if so, would he try and find her? And if he did, would she go with him?

He was all man, but sometimes a woman needed more than that.

With Ryan, she would have someone she could look up to, but she'd be looking up wearing sackcloth for a good long time.

She was sure she could guide him to making a lot of money, some way or other, but how long would it take?

She had a man with money, and if Ryan killed him, which he was likely to do, she could always find another. She'd have to think on it.

Ryan pushed the animals at a hard gallop for almost fifteen minutes, busting brush, happy he had a good pair of *chapaderos.* He pushed them down a long slope, then up another, until he found a spot to rest them in the shade of a rock outcropping.

His leg was not totally healed, and he worried that it would break open again. He kept it bound with tent cloth.

Dismounting, he let the animals blow,

and climbed the face of the rock until he could see his back trail for over a mile.

Now there were only four of them, but they were coming hard.

The good news was they would ride their tired horses down in a hurry, as he knew they'd been pushing much harder than he had through the morning hours.

The bad was they each led another strong-looking mount, and the two in the lead were still the Indians.

He might outdistance them, but unless he dug way up his sleeve for some tricks, he wouldn't lose them.

The northernmost Superstition Mountains rose to the east of them, and the very high Mazatzal Peak and North Mountain to the northwest. He decided to work his way deep into the rugged mountains on the lower Superstition side. Mountains of hard sandstone in deep canyons where, with luck, he couldn't be easily tracked.

He might have a chance of losing even Indian trackers in the Superstitions, if he didn't turn into a box canyon and find himself trapped like a rat in a near-empty grain bin, or worse.

But with only four of them, each with a fresh mount, the tide had turned in their favor.

The dun and the mule were still breathing heavily when he remounted, and both were dripping lather, thick on their withers and flanks. But he had no choice, and gave the dun his heels. The game horse got his legs under him, and in moments they set a trail-eating lope.

Suddenly, he felt as if he was riding for his life.

Thirteen

He was deep in a shaded canyon when he noticed a long gentle sandstone cleft rising to what appeared to be a ridge.

Having no idea if the other side was a gentle slope back to the desert floor or a sharp-shouldered cliff that would trap him, he slowed the dun to a brisk walk and turned him upward.

In moments they were out of the shade and on the gentle rise, dodging the occasional prickly pear until the slope gave way to pure sandstone and hooves rang and echoed in the desert silence.

The cleft became steeper near the top where it funneled into a narrow passage, again shaded.

Topping the little pass, he was pleased to see a long sandy, sparse sage-and-cactus-covered slope dropping back to the desert floor.

An easy, fast escape route.

He found a spot where the animals could be shaded by the higher sides of the pass, dropped reins, grabbed his Winchester, and made his way back on foot to where he could see clearly three hundred yards back down the narrowing cleft.

Sitting up behind a natural rock wall on the west side of the canyon, positioned where the afternoon sun would be in the eyes of his pursuers, he waited.

His wait was rewarded shortly. The two Indians were well ahead of the other two riders.

They had changed mounts, leaving the paints with the following men, he presumed. One now rode a muscled buckskin and the other a tall bay with white feet.

He let them close to a hundred yards, both of them with heads down, concentrating on the hoof scratches in the sandstone that told of his passing. Their horses' hooves now rang, echoing down the cleft.

Having no interest in killing a man trying only to feed his family by earning a few dollars, he leveled the Winchester where he'd take the buckskin mid-chest, and fired.

The rifle bucked in his hand, and for a moment he thought he'd missed as the animal leapt forward. But then the buckskin folded, throwing the Indian over his head, tumbling on the hard sandstone. The horse tried to get up as the Indian did, but the man was obviously knocked senseless as he stumbled in circles. And the horse, down on his hindquarters, merely struggled without gaining his feet.

The second Indian had dived from his horse and scrambled out of sight into the shade of the west side of the canyon, out of Ryan's view.

His horse ran only a few feet, then stood perplexed by the buckskin trying to rise, then falling back.

It almost brought bile to Ryan's throat, having to shoot down a pair of gallant animals whose only sin was doing what their masters bade, but survival dictated and he leveled the .44/40 on the chest of the bay, and again the rifle bucked in his hands.

The bay went up on his rear legs and over, crashing down on his back, not moving.

Ignoring the easy shot at the stumbling man, Ryan scrambled away, regathered his own animals, and set a steady lope down the sandy, sage-and-rock-strewn slope north.

It would be a good long while before the posse regrouped and tried to get to him in the narrow cleft.

If he knew pursuers, they'd work the

canyon on foot, climbing high to peer down on his location, not risking a hard charge through a narrow cleft at a well-entrenched enemy, even though he was only one man.

He'd proven one thing to them, that he was a fair hand with a rifle.

A careful reconnoiter, that's what Ryan would have done, what any sensible man would do.

With luck, it would be near nightfall before they had the confidence to ride after him.

The country was easing the further north he traveled. Tomorrow, as he climbed higher toward the Mogollon Plateau, he would be able to see pines lining the distant mountains. Green grass, and running water.

He smiled as he wiped the dripping perspiration off his brow.

Twice that day he'd stopped and switched the pack and riding saddles, changing animals, allowing one to carry the lighter pack, burdening one with his two hundred pounds.

The first dry meadow he came to, even though it was without water, he stopped, dismounted, wet the horse's and mule's gullets with a hatful of water, and let them graze for fifteen minutes, giving them another hatful each before he mounted and continued on.

By nightfall, he still had seen no sign of the posse. He decided he'd make a cold camp, get up at midnight, and move on. Then he'd rest again at dawn.

By the light of an almost full moon, he resaddled, then was surprised to find the mule favoring his left front leg.

Seeing that the animal had thrown a shoe and picked up an inch-long sharp shard of stone, he dug it out with his knife, but worried that the frog was deeply cut and bruised.

He had an extra shoe and nails, but it was fitted to the horse, not the mule's smaller feet.

He decided to let the mule find his own way, and sure enough the animal followed without the lead rope, but after they'd ridden less than two hours, the gimpy animal began falling behind.

The third time he had to rein up the dun to let the mule catch up, he dismounted and took only the most essential of what the mule carried, rolled it in his bedroll on the dun, hung the canteens on the saddle horn, and discarded the packsaddle and canvas panniers.

If the mule managed to follow, good enough.

If not, he could return to his ancestors, finding a home among the wild burros of the desert.

By dawn the mule, limping badly, was well out of sight behind them.

He was now down to riding one animal, and if the posse was still on his tail, that could mean trouble. But they too were less. Four men, if the Indian who'd taken the bad fall could ride, and now only six horses — the odds were getting better. And they would be a hell of a lot more careful about riding into any place where a man could hole up and get them in a clear field of fire.

As he saddled, he admired the distant ridges to the north and Mazatzal Peak to the west; jagged skylines of tall green pines. Cool forests, cold streams.

To his great pleasure, the mule limped up just as he was about to give his heels to the dun.

He dismounted, and having already watered the dun with half of his last canteen of water, gave the mule the other half, only wetting his own lips as the promise of water lay ahead.

With luck, it was only a half day's ride

up the dry bed he now followed to where Tonto Creek ran cold and clear, then up it another half day to Rancho Conejo, and Felicia.

And, of course, Don Nico Luis Vaca.

Nico allowed Felicia to be driven in the carriage, its small space behind the cushioned seat filled with baggage and hatboxes, while he rode in the lead on one of his finest Andalusian stallions.

They'd camped one night on the banks of the East Verde, then had left well before sunup, much to Felicia's chagrin. It was a two-day ride — before sunup to well after sundown — to the red canyons and cool cottonwood stands of Rio Verde.

Nearby was Fort Verde, where the stage company, working the Prescott-to-Phoenix run, maintained a fine station with not only guest rooms, but a couple of decent cabins on the banks of a clean stream. They were exhausted by the time they arrived.

Felicia, even though she'd been driven and enjoyed the springy ride of the buggy's upholstered seat and shade of its canvas top, was totally wrung out with the dust and heat — but thrilled with the prospect of a roof over her head.

Exhausted, she bathed in a leather tub in the log cabin in hot water, then went straight to bed while Nico and Paco, her driver, enjoyed a bowl of stew, a bowl of frijoles, tortillas, and a bottle of *pulque* in the stage station, and played whist with some soldiers from the fort.

Nico was more than a little drunk and amorous when he finally came to join her, but she feigned being asleep and would not awake to even his most vigorous and insistent shaking. Disgusted, he fell into a deep snoring sleep beside her, reeking of *pulque* or *aguardiente*.

As she listened to the soft water flowing over rocks just outside the waxed-paper window of the cabin, she wondered if Ryan O'Rourke would await them in Prescott by the time they arrived late tomorrow.

And what she would do if he did.

A woman could do worse than having men fight over her, so long as she did not suffer from the experience.

And she did not plan to.

Ryan had moved away from the creek bottom to follow the south rim of the canyon when he thought he was nearing the buildings of Rancho Conejo. More and more he saw a few cattle grazing the

166

slopes, but luckily he'd avoided running into vaqueros.

He was sure most of the don's cattle had been driven to the high country, where summer graze was much better. For the last day and a half he'd seen nothing of the posse, and at night the mule had again caught up with them.

He'd been able to renew the animals' strength with good grass along the creek banks, and they seemed to enjoy the clear water of Tonto Creek as much as he.

He'd even paused to take advantage of a cool pool to wash the grit out of his joints, but now the creek was behind them and they were again in mesquite, scattered with a few dry dusty pines braving the lower climes.

He had actually been on Rancho Conejo one time before, as the guest of Nico Vaca.

When he was still in good stead with Vaca and Boyd he'd been invited, along with other territorial marshals and the circuit judge, to hunt elk in the canyons to the north.

During that trip, Vaca had offered him a stipend of fifty dollars a month, almost as much as Ryan made from the territorial government, since he was "doing such a fine job." His refusal of what he considered a bribe was the beginning of his falling out of favor with Vaca and Boyd. He'd often wondered if other marshals, maybe even the judge, had accepted the same kind of arrangement.

Judge Willard had not imposed the sentence on Ryan that Boyd and Vaca had bragged he would receive, hanging by the neck until dead, and in fact had seemed reluctant to even give him the two years he'd received. So he doubted if the judge was on their payroll — if he had been, Ryan would surely be worm food by now — but he wasn't as confident that his old boss, Hatch Stinman, was not receiving the "stipend" as Vaca had called it.

Clyde Hatcher Stinman had stayed as far from the courtroom as he could during Ryan's trial. During the two-day trial, the marshal had actually come to Ryan in jail to tell him he thought he was getting railroaded, but he'd also done nothing to prevent it.

Another sin of omission as far as Ryan was concerned.

He wasn't on Ryan's vengeance list, but if he got in the way . . .

So just as a full moon disappeared behind the mountains to the west, at three a.m., Ryan sat on the south ridge overlooking the valley where the half dozen rancho buildings huddled in a grove of cottonwood and river willow along Tonto Creek, and although it had been almost four years, he was not unfamiliar with the layout.

There were no lights at the hacienda, not that he expected there would be.

As he eyed the place, he searched his mind for what he knew of the rancho and its vaqueros.

He had hunted with a hard man — Montez was his name if memory served, the man the deputy, Metzler, had mentioned.

Montez, he recalled, had a reputation as a killer, but he had generally done what was asked of him by his boss, Vaca. One time, a year or more later, Ryan had been called to a saloon in Prescott, where Montez had pistol-whipped a drunk, Toby McCantlon.

Ryan had been about to arrest Montez, knowing that Toby was harmless if ignorant — an arrest Ryan felt would result in a gunfight — when Nico Vaca and Ryan's boss, Hatch Stinman, had walked in.

Hatch had allowed Vaca to take Montez out of there, and out of town.

Ryan had called his boss down for the incident, but had been ordered to keep his nose in his own business and out of Hatch's. Hatch had said that there were more important things to which Ryan was not privy.

To Ryan, more important things meant Hatch was beholden to Vaca.

Ryan was still angry over the incident, and Toby had never been quite right since, not that he was a great example of intelligence before.

Even though Ryan hadn't been there when the whipping occurred, and was only called after the fact, he was sure that Toby had done little or nothing to deserve the vicious beating.

But no man in the place would stand up against Montez; for some reason all had been looking the other way while a dozen blows fell on the pudgy little man.

But Ryan did know that Montez was a man with no backup in him, and he had many more hard men behind him who rode for the brand.

He carefully let the dun pick his way down a long slope to the valley bottom. The mule still followed, his leg now almost without any limp.

It was a rich place where subterranean springs fed the first deep and nutritious grass the animals had seen since they'd left the banks of the Tonto, and Ryan was tolerant, letting the horse take a mouthful whenever he wanted, until they rode up and reined up behind what Ryan remembered was the *matanza,* the slaughterhouse and smokehouse.

It was the furthermost building from the hacienda, and near a fairly deep cut that flanked the creek. He was able to ride the last two hundred yards out of sight of any building other than the *matanza.*

A pair of hounds met them, barking wildly, but no lights appeared. If anyone heard, it would be put off to the hounds doing their job, running off coyotes or coons.

The smell of meat smoking made his mouth water, but it was not food that consumed his thoughts at the moment. Across a wide plaza was the *establo* and next to it a common house for the vaqueros. Somewhere there would be Montez and many more hard men with rifles, *pistolas,* and reatas. Only fifty paces away was the veranda wall of the hacienda, and possibly, only steps from that, Felicia McCall slept.

Did she sleep in her own room, or in the room of her "protector," Nico Vaca? Or was she even here?

He would soon know.

Fourteen

The dogs continued to yap, but from a distance of twenty feet, unwilling to close with him.

He carried both the Winchester and the revolver, and slipped into the *matanza* and helped himself to a rope of sausages in casings, but only stuffed a couple in his pocket, then moved out.

He tore one sausage off the rope and flung it to the dogs, who immediately ceased their yapping and went for it. Seeing its success, he tore the rope of more than twenty in half, flinging one half-looping one way, the second the other. Both dogs broke for one string and a tug of war was on. But the yapping had stopped.

He edged around the *matanza* in the darkness and studied the wall and the hacienda beyond.

In the starlight, his eyes made something out in the distance, a hundred or more paces beyond the common house, and it gave him a thought. A way to get the men away from the hacienda, and to keep them away for a good long time.

Returning to the creek bed, he circled the buildings, following it upstream until he judged the distance correct, and climbed up.

What he had seen was now much closer.

A huge stack of meadow hay, forty feet wide and probably well over a hundred long.

Making his way across the mown pasture, he inspected it. Dry as Maricopa Flats. Making a little indentation in the base of the stack, he scratched a lucifer.

When he was confident he would soon have a conflagration, he broke and ran, but the other way this time. To a position that would take him behind the common house.

He only had to wait a moment, seeing that there would be plenty to keep the vaqueros busy. Then he banged on a shutter of the common house and yelled, *"Fuego! Fuego! El heno!* The hay, she burns! *Fuego!"*

In seconds he could hear voices inside the building, and the sounds of scrambling as men came awake and jerked on pantaloons and boots.

He broke and ran until he reached the

rear of the hacienda, away from the hay-stack, which was now roaring, and silhou-etting the buildings.

The wall surrounding the adobe house was higher than Ryan's head, but it was covered with vines. In moments he was looking over its tile-lined top.

There were still no lanterns lit in the ha-cienda, at least none he could see, al-though most of the windows had shutters closed.

The *cocina,* the kitchen, was a separate building from the rest of the hacienda, so fire in the kitchen, the most common place for one to begin, would not travel to the main house. It too was cold and silent, but its shutters were not closed.

It was a cool night, but not cool enough to close shutters, unless part of the house was closed off.

He vaulted the wall and made his way to a wing of the house that he thought he re-membered was the *jefe*'s, the *haciendado*'s, Nico Vaca's.

But the two-inch-thick shutters were barred from the inside.

He'd have to find another way in.

Montez had quarters above the barn, private and far more roomy than the common house. He heard the men yelling below as they passed at a dead run, and was quickly dressed. Halfway to the haystack, he suddenly slid to a halt. The men were setting up a bucket brigade from the creek, but he didn't join in. Instead, he spun on his heel and returned to his room, climbed his stairs, and strapped on a pair of fine Colt *pistolas.*

It was possible for hay to self-combust, not uncommon, in fact. But Señor Vaca had warned him that the *hombre,* Ryan O'Rourke, was *el cazador,* the hunter, and not for elk this time.

Señor Vaca believed he would most likely come to the hacienda, and he would be hunting the *jefe,* and possibly the woman.

And, Montez reasoned, he might just cause a distraction, such as the haystack fire. *That might be what I would do,* Montez thought, *if I were one man among many enemies.*

Montez crossed the yard and slipped into the hacienda veranda through its big carved gates.

Standing quietly for a moment, he studied the adobe house and the windows.

The great room faced him, and its windows flanking the big carved door were glass. Very expensive glass, which the *jefe* had carefully transported all the way from Phoenix.

The only portion of the house that was locked was the *jefe*'s personal quarters, and then only when Vaca was off the rancho as he was now. It would have a padlock on its door, and the shutters would be barred from the inside.

The hacienda was constructed as an H, with the great room and its huge walk-in fireplace and dining room, with a long table seating twenty-four, in the center, and the *jefe*'s private quarters to the right of the entrance. The wing to the left contained guest quarters in the front and servants' quarters in the rear.

Two old ladies and one of their grandsons lived in the rear of the guest wing in three rooms off a little sitting area, the closest part of the hacienda to the *cocina,* where a good portion of their work was performed.

The Vaca family, a wife, eight children, and two surviving parents, along with aunts, uncles, and cousins of three generations, lived on Rancho Cara de la Reina, far to the south on the border with Mexico, the country of the Papago Indians and the great organ-pipe cactus.

Montez moved into the great room, walked to a very dark front corner, leaned against the wall, made sure both his *pistolas* were loose in their holster, and waited in silence.

Ryan was surprised there seemed to be no movement in the main house, but decided he had to get inside to make sure neither Vaca nor Felicia was in residence.

Moving to the side of the hacienda, he came to a room that had the shutters open and slipped through.

With only starlight to guide him, he assessed the room. It seemed to be a small bedroom, with a chest, a bed, and a washstand with a white bowl and pitcher. No one occupied the bed.

He moved to the pitcher and hoisted it. Waterless.

It must be an empty guest room.

The door, heavy wood planking with iron straps, was closed. He worked the latch, opened it to the accompaniment of the loud squeal of iron on iron, then stood for a moment, listening.

He heard another door moan, and light flooded the hallway. He slunk back into the bedroom, but stayed flat against the wall next to the open door.

"Espera, mi hijo. Volvere." Wait, my son. I will return. It was the worried voice of an old woman.

But who was "my son"?

"Sí, abuela." Yes, Gandmother. The voice of a young man, hardly more than a child.

Ryan heard shuffling down the hall, the old woman coming to find out what all the commotion outside was about.

He decided he could use her, and let her pass, then stepped out silently and followed as she turned through an opening and light flooded the great room.

He'd been there before, and it came back to him. He stayed a dozen paces behind her, and reached the opening, just as a deep voice rang out from inside the room.

"Señora Vasquez?"

"Sí, Señor Montez. Qué es la confusión?"

"Fuego en el campo." Fire in the field, he answered.

Ryan stepped through the doorway, his Smith and Wesson hanging loosely in one hand, the Winchester in the other, and Montez snapped his head toward him.

He asked, "Chacho?" It must have been the grandson's name.

"No, Montez, it is not Chacho."

The man did not draw, but merely stood.

Then his voice rang with derision. "You are not welcome here, *gringo*."

"Let's let Vaca tell me that."

"Ha, Señor Vaca is traveling, as is Señorita McCall. You have come for nothing."

Ryan was disappointed, and believed him.

"Quién es?" the old woman asked.

Montez smiled. *"Señor O'Rourke, un bandito,"* he said.

The old woman blanched, but Montez smiled even more broadly.

"I came only to take the life of the scum you call *jefe*," Ryan snapped, angry that the man's boss was not home. "If you'll be so kind as to finger those revolvers out, lay them on that chair, and move away, I'll carry them outside and leave them in the yard as I take my leave."

But Montez made no move to do so. "There is the matter of a fire in the haystack, *gringo*. A fire that could make us short of feed in the winter. If you destroy Vaca property, you hang. That is our law here on Rancho Conejo."

"I guess I'll forgo that entertainment," Ryan said, returning the smile.

"Abuela?" a voice rang out behind Ryan.

Ryan spun, realizing as he did so that it was the voice of the young man, only trying to find his grandmother.

Almost as quickly as he could turn his head and snap it back, he saw Montez reaching for his pistols.

Ryan dove to the side, at the same time bringing his revolver up.

The flash and roar of gunshots filled the air in the darkened room.

Ryan rolled, finding himself under a table.

Another shot came from where Montez had crouched in the corner.

Ryan returned fire, and the old woman screamed, dropping the lantern and running.

There was silence for a moment, but the lantern had burst on the floor, and flames spread, lighting the room.

Montez had one pistol still in hand, but the hand was raised, covering a wound in his upper chest. His eyes were closed, and he winced.

"I am badly wounded," he managed.

"Then throw the weapon aside. I have no reason to kill you, although my old friend Toby McCantlon will be very disappointed."

"He is an *idiota*. No loss," Montez said, but did throw the weapon across the room.

"He's not what he was before you beat him like he was a cur dog, like the coward you are. You're the *idiota,* Montez, if you think making me angry will bode well for you.

"But I guess that hole in your chest is a decent trade . . . particularly if you die like the dog you are."

Ryan rose and walked over and picked up both weapons. He paused in the doorway the way he'd come in. There was no sight of the old woman or her grandson.

"You best ride, *hombre,*" Montez said through gritted teeth, "for my men will have heard the shots. And they know this rancho as they know the breasts of their women."

"I doubt if they heard a damn thing. If you live long enough, tell your *jefe* that I will return, that he doesn't have enough vaqueros to keep him from my bullets. Tell him to pray to the Virgin Mary each night, and to sleep with one eye open . . . as he will rest well soon . . . asleep for all eternity."

"Oh, I will live, *gringo*. I will live to see your tongue feed the crows while you hang at the end of my reata, after I have dragged you through a few miles of cactus. I will live to bring your head to Señor Vaca."

Ryan merely laughed, then disappeared through the doorway as the flames were beginning to spread.

"Señora!" He heard Montez yelling for the old woman.

He was pounding back up to the top of the ridge, the haystack flaming as high as the treetops in the valley below, just as the first light began to silhouette the mountains to the east.

He paused on a ridge almost a mile away.

It was not too far to see men abandoning the haystack and running for the hacienda, as flames were licking out of its roof.

But even as busy as they were at the moment, he was sure that there would soon be two dozen hard-riding vaqueros pounding after him. There were no better horsemen anywhere in the world, and Ryan knew that well, having been to many a rodeo and seen many a vaquero at work on the ranchos.

He was sure he couldn't outride them, but, God willing and the creek don't rise, he could outsmart them.

But what the hell, running was getting to

be a way of life. Not one he treasured, however.

And the odds seemed to be getting worse and worse, but that too seemed to be his lot in life.

Fifteen

It was well after dark when Nico Vaca, Felicia McCall, and her driver, Paco, clomped down the main street of Prescott.

They went straight to Lee Boyd's Arizona Palace Hotel and took adjoining suites on the fourth floor. Paco would sleep in the hayloft of the hotel's livery, which backed up to the hotel and faced the street behind.

As soon as they registered, Felicia demanded a hot bath, even though the clerk informed her that the bathwater, heated in a huge cauldron in the kitchen, was without a fire for the rest of the night.

He suggested she have a tub and hot water delivered to her room in the morning.

"I will sleep the morning through, my good man, and I'll not retire with this road dirt in every crack and cranny of my being."

"It's a great deal of trouble," the officious little man said, looking down his nose at her.

Even Nico was tired, and wanted to be in his room. But not too tired to anger quickly.

He slapped his quirt on the desktop, the crack of it reverberating through the lobby, making the man jump as if he'd been shot.

"Not so much trouble as me whipping you raw. Not so much trouble as Señor Boyd having you tarred and feathered and ridden out of town on a rail. Do as she asks. And do it now."

The man's voice trembled as he slunk against the back wall. "Of course, Señor Vaca, I meant no offense."

"Then *vaya* for *la agua,* after you give us our keys and we *vamos* . . . to our rooms."

He ran from the lobby.

When they reached the rooms, she entered hers and he his, but he immediately walked to the connecting door and banged on it, as it was latched from both sides.

She answered, taking down her hair.

"You will be bathed and in my bed when I return. I'm going to find Lee Boyd."

She was too tired to argue. "I will be, but try and not wake me."

"I will wake you, *querida.*" He smiled tightly, slapping the quirt on his thigh as if it was a threat, then spun on his heel and left.

He found Boyd sitting at the only table

on the balcony of his Sundown Saloon, watching the players and drinkers below. He was huddled with McManus Peters, the manager of his Tempest Opera House.

Boyd introduced them, then told Peters, "If you don't mind, Mac, we have some private business."

The man doffed his hat and disappeared down the stairway.

"So, Vaca, I trust your trip was easy?"

"Hot as hell, as usual. What have you heard of Señor O'Rourke?"

"He was in Phoenix, where he went to the bank and picked up a hundred-dollar draft."

Vaca stared, incredulous. "And he was not detained? Did they not know of the wanted poster?"

"They did." Boyd smiled. "He didn't exactly go to the bank during business hours. He escorted the bank president there at gunpoint."

"So he's wanted for that offense?"

"Nope. The banker didn't press charges. And O'Rourke didn't steal anything. Only took what was coming to him."

Vaca sighed deeply. "So you and I will have to kill him, if he's not smart enough to use the money to take the train somewhere far distant."

Boyd shrugged his heavy shoulders.

"What will be, will be," Boyd said. He smiled, but a little like a cat at a canary. "I've got a half dozen hard men on the lookout for him, as well as every territorial marshal in the territory. I doubt if we'll have the chance to shoot him down. Hang him maybe, but he'll be behind bars long before he can get face-to-face with either of us."

"I need a drink, *amigo*."

Boyd walked to the railing and shouted down to a bartender over the plinking of a piano.

"Hey, Swartzy, get one of the girls to bring up a bottle of the good stuff, and two glasses."

He returned to the table and sat, giving his partner a reassuring smile.

"He won't be a problem. By the way, I've got the stage-side box reserved for you and Felicia every night for the next week, and we've got a full calendar of great entertainment."

In moments, they were toasting to Ryan O'Rourke's pending hanging, and then to other business.

They spent the next two hours talking, but Ryan's name did not come up again.

Felicia was feigning being asleep when

Nico returned, seemingly drunk, as he dropped his boots to the floor . . . but he would not be denied.

He shook her and called her name several times, then physically turned her to her back.

"Please, Nico," she managed to murmur in complaint.

"*Es verdad, querida,* you will be pleased."

Ryan rode hard all through the morning.

The mule was no longer limping, so he traded the saddle and bridle and changed mounts four times, keeping up a canter, no matter how steep the trail.

The trail out of the valley to the west was easy to follow, marked with the tracks of a very light wagon, or more likely a buggy, as the tires were less than an inch wide. He imagined that Felicia had been the reason for that buggy, and pushed even harder knowing in his heart that he was getting closer and closer to her with every step. And in finding her, the bonus would be Nico Vaca.

He stayed on the track until he thought he spied dust in the distance behind him; a lot of dust, a lot of riders.

The first trickle of water he came to after

seeing the dust plume was a three-foot-wide creek with a shale bottom. He carefully eyed the trail, noting the tracks of several shod horses other than his own animals.

He rode past the creek a hundred yards, then swung off the trail onto some hardpan, heading to the south until he came to a rock ridge, then followed it back down to the trickle.

Turning north in the little stream, he crossed the road, this time his tracks unseen in the hard shale of the creek bottom, and followed the stream upward into the ponderosas.

It was natural to assume a man, or animal, being pursued, would take the route upon which he could move the fastest, the downhill route. He hoped his pursuers would make that mistake about his selection of a path of escape. He stayed in the creek bottom as long as he felt it was doing any good to hide his trail, then, after a mile, broke back to the west, where he saw what looked to be a pass over the next ridge.

Crossing the ridge, he found himself on a rimrock and had to work his way on top of the ridge further north, until the cliff lessened and he was able to pick his way back into the trees below.

Over a mile to the south he spotted the ever-moving dust cloud. Well past the creek. He'd fooled them, outsmarted them, at least for the moment.

Now he had to make sure he stayed well off the trail, and well out of sight of the riders below.

The riding, following only game trails, was much harder, but surely much safer.

He stopped to graze the horses in a couple of meadows before he again rode into the high desert; on a line drawn by God, cool pines were replaced by tall cactus and mesquite.

Confident he was as well hidden in the mesquite as he was in the pines, he pressed on.

He dined that night, near to midnight, in a cold camp in a tight mesquite thicket that would be impossible to penetrate without making noise, feasting on the two sausages he'd borrowed from Rancho Conejo.

Late the following day, after pushing hard, he saw smoke in the distance. After a mile of picking his way through the cactus and sage, he came to the edge of a high rimrock.

It was time to rest and change mounts, so he tied the animals in the sparse shade of a stand of tall mesquite, and trying to determine the source of the smoke, moved to the edge of the rimrock on foot.

And he was glad he had. The main road was in a canyon below, and less than a half mile from where he crouched in the rocks was a group of less than a dozen buildings. Camp Verde, a small town, where the stage company kept a station.

The smoke actually came from the north, where Fort Verde sat well away from the Rio Verde, and a half mile below the mouth of Beaver Creek. He was back in civilization, the first he'd seen since Phoenix, unless you considered Rancho Conejo to be civilized.

Ryan preferred to think of anything connected to Nico Vaca as being heathen, with the one exception, of course, of Felicia McCall.

Speaking of Nico Vaca, he wondered if the don and his buggy, and Felicia, might be in Camp Verde.

Maybe he would reconnoiter the town after nightfall. The buggy should be easy to find.

He decided to take his chances and rest until after sundown. Watering the animals and himself with the canteens, he dozed in the shade, until he heard the echoing sounds of a cadre of riders beating the road below. Again, he made his way to the edge of the rimrock.

He got a belly chuckle. Over twenty vaqueros, and four more riders he didn't expect. The posse, all the way from Phoenix, had teamed up with the rancho riders.

He was beginning to feel as popular as the only pork chop in a camp of hungry men.

Jesus and Mary, he wondered how much had been placed on his head to bring them this far.

Almost smug that he was worth so much — at least his head on a platter was — he returned to his shady spot and dozed until he heard the chipping of crickets replacing the hum of cicadas in the brush.

He stood and stretched, then resaddled. One thing was sure. He wouldn't be taking the main road over the pass into the Cottonwood Valley and on to Prescott.

And, he decided, the fact that the vaqueros and the posse had passed on through Camp Verde assured him that Nico Vaca was not there.

Ryan was sure that Vaca was on his way to Prescott, where he had many business interests. Had he been headed south to his other ranchos, he would have followed Tonto Creek, not taken the pass over the mountain to Camp Verde.

No, Prescott was Ryan's best bet, and now he didn't have to risk a ride through the ramshackle town of Camp Verde.

The early evening moon was helpful, as he had to follow the rimrock until he found a place to pick his way down to Rio Verde. A small creek provided that pathway.

He knew that somewhere between Camp Verde and Fort Verde, the road branched, with one branch north to Navajo country and the other northwest to Prescott. He couldn't risk the road, but he could risk taking Beaver Creek. He'd run a man to ground on Beaver Creek a few years back, a half-breed who'd murdered a miner, and Ryan knew the country fairly well.

There was more than one clear spring up the mountain from Rio Verde, and he figured to ride up the Beaver to the higher elevations, where he'd find good grass and fresh water.

He did so without consequence, camping by a free-flowing spring that fed Beaver Creek and one of its willow-branch-dammed ponds.

He went to bed hungry, although the horses had plenty of fodder.

But his stomach flapping against his backbone mattered little.

Tomorrow night, he'd be in Prescott.

Of course, so would twenty angry vaqueros and a posse who'd been dogging his trail for more than a hundred miles, and more than likely a mess of hard men hired by Leander Boyd.

By tomorrow night, he'd be feeling like a shoat in a den of wolves.

But tonight, life was good, even though dinner was the last stick of jerky, no more than a couple of ounces, and a crumbled biscuit.

Sixteen

Morning came early up on the mountain, and Ryan, without coffee or grub, had no reason to linger.

Besides, he was eager and anxious to get to Prescott to see what awaited him.

At least his animals were well grazed and watered.

He could see the light on the top of Mingus Mountain just south of where he dropped into Cottonwood Canyon. He wasn't halfway down the mountain he'd used to overnight on when he noticed the dun hesitate and his ears go up.

He'd taken to carrying the Winchester in the saddle scabbard and the Smith and Wesson in his belt, and he made sure the rifle rode light and the revolver was not jammed so far in his belt that it would hang up if it had to be jerked.

After another fifty feet, he saw the top of a sombrero over a stand of buck brush, and reined up, watching carefully.

But the sombrero rode atop a man who

rode atop a walking horse, and they continued out on the trail, seemingly unaware of Ryan's presence.

"Good morning," Ryan called out, as it was too late to rein off the trail and let the man pass.

He pulled rein.

A heavyset vaquero, on the trail alone. A bedroll on the back of the saddle seemed to indicate he was traveling. The man casually rested his hand on the butt of his revolver, as did Ryan. It was not an aggressive move, only a cautious one.

The fat vaquero doffed his hat with his other hand.

"Buenos dias, amigo."

Then he narrowed his eyes, then removed his hand from the butt of his revolver.

"By the saints, if it is not Señor O'Rourke."

Ryan was a bit taken aback, but the man seemed friendly enough.

"Yes, and you're . . . ?"

"Innocente . . . Innocente Alverez Robles. You remember, Señor. We rode together to catch that dog of a miner who killed *mi amigo,* Juan Flores."

Ryan scratched his head for a minute; then it came back to him. He smiled at the grinning man.

"I do remember. We chased that hombre all the way to the Santa Maria River, halfway to California. How could I forget, *amigo?*"

"Ayi-yi-yi, we did and we caught him, and to my *paisano*'s great surprise and pleasure, your judge hanged him in the town square."

"Almost five years ago," Ryan said.

"And you, *amigo,* you have been in the *gringo juzgado?*"

"I have, and hoosegow is much too nice a word for that dung-beetle hole, but I'm a free man now."

"Let's sit a spell and talk of it," the Mexican offered.

"I would like that, Señor Robles, but I'm out of grub and on my way to Prescott. My gut is growling like a grizzly on the prowl."

The fat man slapped his belly. "You think an *hombre gordo* like me is on the trail without frijoles and tortillas? I have a satchel full of pork and some *salsa caliente. Poco tiempo, poco tiempo.* Climb down, *amigo,* and we will talk of friends past, and new friends to be made."

Ryan was anxious to be on the trail, but his stomach overruled his eagerness.

He also had no idea when and where he might find another meal.

He remembered riding with this man, who, although full-girthed, had outlasted another deputy and a posse of a half dozen townspeople in pursuit of the miner.

He'd been a good reliable partner on the trail.

Ryan smiled. "How can I turn down an offer of something that will probably scald my gut from toothy entrance to toothless exit?"

The big man laughed hardily. "I desired *desayuno,* and now I have the excuse."

The big man swung his bulk off the skunk-stripped dun he rode, unstrapped his bedroll, and walked into the shade of a pine.

Ryan moved his animals into the shade, loosened their girths, and followed to where Innocente Alverez was unrolling his gear and removing some tin containers and a bottle.

"Pulque?" the big man asked.

But Ryan had brought along one of his recently filled canteens and he shook his head.

"No, sir. I got a full day. And *pulque* will turn me off the trail toward siesta."

"So, *amigo,* tell me . . . is this *juzgado* in Yuma the rat hole as I have been told?"

They talked as they ate, and as Ryan suspected, the salsa, even when mixed with the pork and wrapped in a tortilla, and chased with a pint of water, scalded his gullet.

Innocente laughed as Ryan gulped the water.

Then he turned serious. "I understand the men with the badge seek you again. You are a very valuable man."

Ryan eyed him cautiously. "So I understand. Is there a poster?"

"There is, five hundred dollars, but it does not say dead or alive."

Ryan laughed. "So, I'm surprised I'm sharing your *desayuno,* and not looking down the barrel of your *pistola.*"

"You were a *gringo* who went after another *norteamericano* who had killed a *mexicano,* a *paisano* of mine. I consider you an *amigo,* and I don't consider many *gringo*s to be such." He eyed Ryan up and down, smiling before he continued. "No, *amigo,* a *gringo* friend of mine, of my *paisanos,* is worth much more than five hundred dollars."

"I'm glad to hear it, Innocente, as I remember you hit what you shoot at."

The big man shrugged, then changed the subject.

"I am going to Fort Verde, to discuss the

199

sale of some horses with the *comandante*. I enjoy riding in the cool of the high country this time of year, even though it is further . . . and besides, I have been advised that the sale of horses to the army is the property of only one man, and that man will not be pleased when I cut his price from fifty to forty dollars.

"There may be men on the main road, to deter me from my journey, if I know my enemies. And you are going where?"

"Prescott, to discuss settling an old score with old friends, who are now . . . and I guess always were, enemies."

"Is Señor Boyd among those you seek?"

"He's on the top of the list, as well as one of your *paisanos*."

"Don Nico Vaca?"

"Yes."

"You have my blessing, *amigo*. Señor Boyd is the man who has advised me not to interfere in his business with the army, and Don Vaca cheated my family out of land and water many years ago. My *desayuno* has been well invested, should you shoot them down in the street."

Innocente rolled his goods, then rose and stretched. "You should know that Señor Boyd has been hiring, and not men who are good with a pick or who can pour an honest drink or turn an honest card. He's been hiring *pistoleros*. Men good with a gun. He has six in his employ, last count."

Ryan shrugged this time, as if it meant little to him. At least he now knew why others were after him with such fervor, and that his adversaries had grown in number. What difference did a few more make? When Vaca and Boyd went away, men dependent upon their purses would disappear like a tendril of smoke in the desert wind. He extended his hand to the big man.

"So I will be busy. And so I may not see you for a long while to pay back this fine meal," Ryan said.

"It is no matter. Stay alive, and I will collect when we both don't have to watch our backs."

They shook, waved their good-byes, and rode in different directions.

It was late afternoon before Ryan spotted Prescott up the hill a mile in front of him.

He reined up in the shade of a cottonwood and let the horse and mule blow. He didn't want to have winded animals, should he have to ride out in a hurry. But they'd have time to rest, as he wasn't about to ride into town in the light of day.

He decided to ride a little closer to town, then swing off the trail to find a shady spot.

He'd gone less than halfway when the dun's ears turned back, and he glanced around as he clomped along. Ryan looked over his shoulder, to see a half dozen riders a quarter mile behind, coming hard, dust flying.

Only hesitating a second, he gave heels to the dun, dragging the mule along behind. After a couple of hundred yards he again looked over his shoulder and estimated the hard-riding bunch to be gaining on him.

Trying to ride with the slower mule dragging behind was too much, so he flung the lead rope, deciding to let the mule find his own way, and hunkered lower in the saddle.

Ahead of him, two large cottonwoods flanked the trail and it made a slight turn. He decided he'd leave the trail just after passing them, although he was not even sure these men were after him.

A pair of gunshots sang over his head, and he was no longer unsure.

He drew within a few feet of the trees and glanced behind one more time, hoping he'd be out of their sight when he veered off into the underbrush.

Had he not turned to eye his pursuers, he might have seen the reata suddenly drawn taut across the road. The dun tried to set his legs to leap, but was too close. The woven leather caught him at mid-leg, and he flipped head over heels.

Ryan slammed hard, barely able to get his hands in front of him. The wind was knocked from him and he gasped, trying to catch his breath. He managed to sit up, just as another reata dropped over him and a rider pounded past, sucking the loop up tight, catching both his arms, then jerking him away as if he were a leaf in a dust devil.

Before he knew it, riders were on either side, pounding hard, as he was slammed one way, then the other, rolling, careening off the hard spots in the road, tangling in and being jerked free of chaparral on the roadside, but always moving forward.

The last thing he remembered was buildings and people all around him, and a vaquero leaning over him, hands on his knees, an evil smile on his face showing tobacco-stained teeth.

"My *segundo,* Montez, told you, *gringo,* you would enjoy the taste of the reata. He was too tough to die with your poor shooting, and cannot ride for a while. But I will describe your ride of the oak horse to him . . . you will dangle from a reata soon."

Then Ryan passed out, again beaten and bruised, wondering if he would ever awake again.

Nico Vaca smiled his serpent-tight-lipped grin at Felicia.

"Well, *querida,* will you go see your old friend in the jail?"

She returned a smile equally reptilian.

"Nico, Nico, when will you believe that Señor Ryan and I were only passing acquaintances? I will be happy to visit him, if that's your wish."

"No, no. I thought you would be eager . . ."

He decided to change the subject.

"It is too bad we won't be here to see him hang."

"Hang? I was under the impression he was only wanted to testify at a hearing, to clear his name."

Nico flushed. "How did you know . . . ?"

Then he smiled tightly again.

"Felicia, my little dove, you should keep your sharp beak to yourself and stay out of others' personal property . . . and affairs."

Felicia smiled at Nico, but her eyes narrowed. "To be told a half-truth, my love, is the same as being lied to. To be purposefully given half a message is the same as being told a half-truth."

He flushed even more. "Are you calling me a liar, Felicia?"

She spun on her heel and left the room, but as she disappeared into her adjoining room, she spoke over her shoulder.

"You lied in court when Ryan was tried. It seems you liked the taste of it."

She slammed the door, and he heard her engage the latch.

He yelled at the door.

"Ah, but he is now wanted for assault and attempted murder. He shot Montez, while he was trying to protect my hacienda . . . your home. You should be happy he'll hang."

She'd stopped short when he began yelling, and called back through the door.

"You don't hang for attempted murder. . . ."

"In the town of Leander Boyd and Nico Vaca you do!"

"And you'll answer to Governor Fremont if he hangs without trial."

"Puta," he mumbled, and walked to the

sideboard and poured himself a shot of Boyd's fine whiskey.

He will hang, for this time we have the judge at our disposal.

Seventeen

Was he in hell? Banshees wailing?

Then he realized it was the back-rattling squeak, a grinding squeal, of a flat-barred door on hinges that had not seen oil in many years.

He felt about and realized he was not six feet under; he was lying on a hard bunk; not a bunk, but a blanket covering stone.

He knew exactly where he was.

He'd been here many times, only outside the bars looking in.

He tried to rise, but every bone and muscle screamed in protest. Taking a deep breath, he realized that muscles where he didn't know he had muscles were complaining. Wondering if he had broken bones, with his eyes still closed, he felt one arm up and down, then reversed the process.

Then he felt the knots and cuts on his head.

Almost so many knots that the only

normal places felt as if they'd been crushed in, and he wouldn't be surprised if some of them had been.

However, he was awake, and angry, so he was probably fine.

Still worrying that he was broken somewhere, he managed to sit up and get his eyes open.

He felt his legs carefully, from thigh to ankle.

Damned if he didn't seem to be in one piece.

His rib cage hurt so bad it was almost more than he could do to prod about, but he decided he had no more than a cracked rib, if that.

He was fine, although he knew that a cracked rib could keep him from enjoying a deep breath for a good long while.

Fine, if you didn't count bruises and scrapes. By the scabs on his head and face, he decided he must have left a good portion of his hide out there in the Prescott street.

"You coming to life?" a voice asked. "You been out all night and through most the morning."

"Such is life, at the moment," he said, then saw a smiling man wearing a badge and carrying a tray, just outside his cell door. He was a barrel-chested fellow, with light hair and fair skin, as tall as Ryan.

"I got a bowl of beans, some sourdough bread, and a glass of cool water here. Towrey's Bakery and Creamery makes the best bread in the territory. And the best ice cream, but you won't be gettin' no ice cream."

"Thanks for bringing it up. I ain't had ice cream in over two years. Can you slip that under the bars and leave it, till I get my wits about me?"

"I can, but I'd better be getting the spoon back or there'll be no chow tomorrow."

Ryan knew the Prescott jail well, and glanced around.

"Let me see, it would take me only about ten years to chip my way through this rock with a spoon. I believe those beans are a better use."

The deputy laughed.

"I'm Joshua Clemmons, Territorial Deputy Marshal . . . your old job, if you're Ryan O'Rourke, and them what's seen you say you are under those knots and scabs."

"I wish I could say pleased to meet you, Josh, but it's a little hard to mouth anything cheerful right now as my jawbone is one of the many things that don't work so good."

"I understand. I'll be back to get the utensils."

He turned to leave, then stopped short.

"You had a visitor this morning. Fella with a fine beard. Said he'd be back in the p.m."

"Who would that be?"

"Levy, I believe he said his name was. He left you a medicine bottle full of some concoction. Said you look like you can use it."

"I can. May I have it?"

He knew Dr. Levy's concoctions, and knew they were ninety proof. Just what he needed to quell the pain at the moment.

"I'll bring it when I pick up the leavings."

Dr. Levy, back from California and Yuma. He'd wasted no time getting back to Prescott. At least Ryan had a friend here in Prescott.

And he had a chore for the good doctor.

But the doctor wasn't his first visitor.

He was less than surprised when Territorial Marshal Clyde Hatcher Stinman walked up to the bars. Ryan was a little drunk on the half pint of ninety-proof medicine.

"How you feelin', Ryan?"

"Like kickin' some Mexican butt all over your street outside."

"You'd better heal some afore you try it. I didn't know if you was gonna wake up, beat up as you are."

"Oh, I'm awake all right. When you gonna let me out of here, Hatch?"

Hatcher laughed, but it was low and a little ominous.

"Don't think that's gonna happen soon. I'd say you'd be lucky not to walk out of here on a short trip to meet thirteen turns in a hemp rope."

Ryan was quiet for a moment, then said, "Well, Hatch, if that's the case, I musta done something real bad while I was knocked out."

"You wasn't knocked out when you attempted to murder Montez, Vaca's foreman over at Rancho Conejo."

"News travels fast. So, he survived? I didn't think me shootin' him near to his shoulder would kill him. He's a tough bird."

"Some other tough old boy rode a day and a half straight through. That's why they was laying for you. Hell, you had half the country looking for you, thanks to a poster printed up and reward offered by Lee Boyd. Montez's laid up, but he'll more than likely fork a cayuse again."

It was Ryan's turn to laugh.

"You know me about as well as any man, Hatch. You think if I'd tried to kill Montez that he'd still be suckin' air? He was shootin' at me and I shot back."

"In Nico Vaca's hacienda, where you wasn't invited. I doubt if self-defense is gonna fly no better than a pig with this one. And I never saw no pig with wings."

Again Ryan was quiet for a spell.

"Is Orval Tisdale still hanging his hat, and shingle, in Prescott?" he finally asked.

"He is, but between you and me, he's in Boyd's shirt pocket."

"How about Peter T. Polkinghorn?"

"He represents Boyd's mines."

"Hell, who else is there?"

"Aluishious Cosgrove."

"Drunk as usual?"

"Nope, some more than usual, I'd guess."

"I need to buy some time before I go to trial. You still gettin' them before Judge Haycock in three days or less?"

"Haycock retired. John Patrick Coleman is the circuit judge these days, but you're in luck."

"How so?"

"He's back in Washington, and it'll be two or more weeks till he's due back . . . so all I got to worry about is keeping the lynch mob cooled down."

Ryan let out a deep sigh of relief.

Then, on second thought, he asked, "Is Coleman in Boyd's pocket too?"

"Can't rightly say," Hatcher said, but his tone revealed what Ryan feared.

"So I don't have the chance of a hen in a fox den?"

"You said it, I didn't."

"Would you ask Cosgrove to call on me?"

"What time's good for you?" Hatcher asked, then guffawed deeply.

"Let me check my schedule. When he's sober, that might be a good time for me. How about real early tomorrow morning?"

"I'll see if the old boy is up to it."

Hatcher hadn't been gone ten minutes when Dr. Aaron Levy's slender form appeared outside the bars.

"How you feeling, Ryan, my lad?"

"That tonic you left me did a world of good. Bring me another couple of bottles if you would. How are you, Doc?"

"Good, just arrived yesterday, in time to see the commotion as they drug you up in front of this fine establishment."

Ryan eyed him quizzically. "You and I still in good stead, Doc?"

"Unless you're a different man than the one I knew in Yuma, we are."

"Then I need a favor."

Levy glanced at the heavy stone walls. "I don't carry dynamite in my list of goods, Ryan."

Ryan smiled, then continued. "Nope, I wouldn't want you in here with me. How about sending a couple of telegrams for me? I'll owe you, unless Marshal Stinman has my money in his safe."

"I doubt that, and I'm not worried about it. What and to whom?"

In moments, Levy was back from the front office, where Joshua Clemmons, Stinman's big deputy, had provided him with a couple of sheets of foolscap and pen, ink, and blotter.

Ryan wrote carefully, only needing one sheet of paper:

To:
Reese Conner, Denver, Colorado
Ethan or Dillon McCabe, Bozeman, Montana
Message:
Seems the railroad is again active here in Prescott, where I'm a guest of the territory.
Sorry to trouble you. Hail to the Kin of Killorglin.

Ryan

He handed the single sheet to Dr. Levy, along with the pen, inkwell, and blotter.

"I kept this short to keep the cost down."

"I told you, lad, it's no matter."

"Matters to me, Aaron. I might not be able to pay you back."

"Rest assured I'll check with the marshal to see if he is holding your funds, and draw from them if he'll allow."

Ryan extended his hand through a narrow slot provided for passing things in and out of the cell.

"I'm obliged, Aaron."

"Ryan, I would say it's my pleasure, but my much greater pleasure would be sitting down to a game of chess or cribbage with you outside this cell."

Ryan smiled tightly.

"You just go ahead and plan on it, Doc."

Aaron Levy nodded and headed out.

"I'll be back, tomorrow at the latest," he called over his shoulder, but he was back in only moments.

"Ryan," he called from the door, "it seems Marshal Stinman has one hundred twenty-seven dollars on account for you. He says he'll make a hundred of it available for your defense or other matters, but the balance will be held for your meals."

"Tell him I said he's an honest man and a true gentleman . . . no matter who he calls friends."

"I believe I'll let you tell him."

Then Aaron was gone, and Ryan returned to his bunk to sleep off the hurt.

Nico Vaca and Leander Boyd enjoyed a breakfast of steak and eggs at Willowby's Café next to Boyd's Palace Hotel, while Boyd read a copy of Ryan's telegram.

After he'd finished, he asked his partner, "What the hell does Ryan care about the railroad possibly coming to town, and who the hell is the Kin of Killorglin?"

Vaca merely shrugged.

So Lee continued. "You know anything of these Conner and McCabe fellows, or this Dr. Levy who sent the telegram at O'Rourke's behest?"

"No," Nico replied, "but it can't be good. How do we hurry up Señor O'Rourke's trial?"

"You got to have a judge for a trial. Fremont is in Washington, and then is visiting relatives somewhere. He could appoint a temporary acting judge . . . but then again, maybe Tobar would?"

"Tovar?"

"No, Tobar. He's the chairman of the assembly, and the acting governor in Fremont's absence."

"And this Tobar, does he owe us his allegiance?" Nico asked.

"Hell, he's got family money and I haven't been able to get next to him. He's damn nigh as unapproachable as Fremont. However, he's a regular customer at one of my brothels. He's taken a shine to a chubby little Slovakian girl there . . . and I imagine he'd as soon his wife didn't learn that little bit of information."

"Then it's worth a try, *amigo?*"

"It's always worth a try, partner. What is it they say? 'You don't get what you don't ask for.' "

Nico laughed. "Señor O'Rourke has."

"True, true. I'll head over to the territorial administration building this afternoon, and we'll see what can be done."

"Good, I would like to see him hang quickly, while Felicia is here to enjoy it."

Boyd smiled, but did not reply. He knew that Vaca was insanely jealous of Ryan O'Rourke; even though O'Rourke was little more than a jailbird, he was a mountain of a man and one whom the ladies admired. He knew, as did Vaca, that O'Rourke and Felicia McCall had been seeing each other on the sly, long before

Polkinghorn, Felicia's former suitor, had been killed by O'Rourke. It had complicated matters somewhat, during O'Rourke's former trial . . . the fact that Polkinghorn had a reason, other than business, to come after O'Rourke.

It had surprised even Boyd when Felicia, after Ryan had been transported to Yuma, had sought Nico Vaca as her "protector."

But O'Rourke had been out of the picture.

Of course, her taking up with Vaca shouldn't have been such a surprise, as Vaca was the richest man in the territory and Felicia the most beautiful woman.

Of course, a snake is beautiful, if you look past the fangs.

And Felicia knew what side her bread was buttered on.

Boyd eyed his tight partner before he spoke. "We need to give your man Aleandro a bonus for riding on ahead of your men . . . riding like the bloody desert wind to get here in thirty hours to tell us O'Rourke was on his way. It was quite a feat."

"Ha, you are sometimes such a *gringo*. It is nothing for a vaquero, even the *gente de razon*."

Boyd smiled, but insisted. "Look, Nico, I'll toss in a ten-dollar gold piece if you will."

"And spoil one of my men? You take care of your employees and I will take care of mine."

"So I don't imagine you intend to honor the poster I had made and pay your men and mine, who dragged him in, the five hundred?"

"They are my employees. They are paid fair wages with each new moon."

Vaca's tight purse often irritated Boyd. "Hell with you, Nico. Information and action is what makes the wheels of my business go round. Ask Aleandro to come see me. I'll at least take care of him."

"As you wish, *gringo,* but you should watch your tongue. You're not speaking to one of your brothel *putas.*"

"That's for damn sure," Boyd said. "You're a lot of things, but sweet and pretty sure ain't none of them."

Eighteen

At noon that same day a delivery boy arrived at Mother Alice's Rooming House in Denver and left a telegram with the chambermaid.

It was late that day — he'd worked almost all night — when Reese Conner awoke, washed up at the bowl and pitcher, dressed, and came downstairs, with his hair slicked and his broad-brimmed bone-white beaver hat under his arm, to head for work at McGuire's, the biggest saloon and gambling establishment serving Denver.

As always, Reese was dressed as well as or better than the most prestigious of Denver's elite, right down to buttoned waistcoat, stiff collar, watch, chain and fob, and diamond stickpin in his four-in-hand tie. His coat was black with black velvet trim and his pants gray pinstriped. He carried a hideout boot gun and a Colt revolver strapped on his hip.

One never knew, in the gambling trade, when a customer might mistake deftness for cheating and take more than mere umbrage at the loss of a hand.

And one thing about McGuire's, it didn't tolerate cheating from customer or house man, but it did allow customers to retain their firearms on their hips and in boots and belts. Men had even been known to lean scatterguns against the bar as they guzzled rotgut.

He was almost out the door before Alice, the buxom elderly proprietress of the establishment, remembered the telegram.

"Mr. Conner," she called out, stuffing a strand of gray hair back under her dust cap. "I didn't want to bother you while you were resting, but you have a telegram."

Reese Conner read the wire, then wadded it up and dropped it on an entry table.

"Alice, lass, please call me Reese. I'll be gone a while on personal business. I trust you'll watch after my things and any mail I might receive?"

She smiled, cutting her eyes down. It had been some years since anyone had called her "lass."

"Of course I will, Mr. Conner."

"Alice, it's Reese. Please, lass. . . ."

He reached up and patted her on a chubby rosy cheek, and it became even more crimson as she blushed. At charming womenfolk he was almost as adept as he was at cards. Digging a pair of twenty-dollar gold pieces out of his pocket, he placed them on the side table.

"This should handle things for a while."

She nodded, looking at him with admiration, then cutting her eyes quickly away as his met hers.

He'd only been in Denver for a couple of months, and had lived in this particular rooming house for a couple of weeks, but he liked the food, the fact that Alice respected his strange hours and willingly fed him at odd times, and the fact his sheets were changed twice a week.

His room was a dormered garret on the third floor, where an enemy couldn't sneak up to his window.

One thing Reese Conner had plenty of was enemies.

His Colt was notched so much he'd decided to replace the oak grips, and wished he'd never taken to notching, for it was an advertisement that attracted the overambitious who wanted a quick reputation.

When asked, he said the notches were for the weasels he'd shot, and that wasn't altogether a lie.

Most of those who'd called him out over

the years had had to be drunk to do so, in order to work up the courage, as Reese was snake-quick and prone to staying alive.

There was little glory in outdrawing a drunken blowhard who couldn't hit his butt with both hands, but killing a man looking for a reputation just compounded Reese's problem; the more he killed, the more ambitious young bucks wanted to make a quick reputation by killing him.

Sometimes Reese wished he could find a place where no one knew or had heard of him.

Ryan, only two years his senior, was his favorite cousin — closer than his own brother — having come to Reese's aid more than once when they were growing up, and later when they were wild and woolly and riding for the Confederacy.

He'd likely lose his job at McGuire's with an extended absence, but that was of little consequence, for kin had called, and kin would come.

He knew one of the other kin was close by.

His brother Ret, actually Garret Loch Conner, who was known as Professor to many as he was the most educated and oldest of this generation of the kin. And had been a teacher until a headmaster's daughter turned up with child and he'd left town just ahead of an angry bunch of her relatives.

Ret was last heard of somewhere in the mountains west of Denver, one of the mining towns.

Reese clamped his jaw at the thought of having to contact Garret, as the two of them hadn't gotten along for years.

But this was kin trouble, and it rose above mere dislike.

As he moved down the street toward his first stop, McGuire's, where he would inform them of his coming absence, up ran the boy from the telegraph office.

He knew the youngster, Eric, and tipped his hat as the boy gave Reese a big grin.

"Mr. Conner, here's another wire for you. You're right popular. Can I take a look at your six-gun while you're reading?"

"Eric, lad, you should be interested in your books, not in sidearms. God willin', by the time you reach your majority, we'll have no need of them on Western streets, and long guns will be used only to put meat in the smokehouse."

The boy looked disappointed as he handed Reese the wire, then elated as Reese dug in his pocket and handed him a dime.

Reese,
Reached Garret by wire in Leadville.
He will join you in Alamosa in two or
three days. Please arrange for some
good mounts as Ethan and I will arrive
Denver in one week by stage.
Reached Kathleen in Albuquerque.
She will join us in Prescott. She will
beat all of us there. You and Garret try
and save your bullets for Ryan's ene-
mies. The Burkes are nowhere to be
found, Fiona will keep trying. I think
the McCreeds are still inside. Seems
time for the kin to raise dust.

Dillon

Dillon always was the organized one, and he knew damn good and well that he and Garret had never come to shootin' at each other, although there'd been many a Katy-bar-the-door bout of fists, kicks, elbows, and gouges.

Reese was sorry Dillon had found Kathleen, for if it was up to Reese, she'd be left out of it.

Her career, her reputation as an actress, was growing, and he knew she would have to cancel some appearances, and would lose a lot of money in the process.

But Ryan was her brother, and the fact

was, she'd be spittin' mad if the kin had not contacted her. And you didn't want wee Kathleen mad at you. And she could be some help, as her stage name was Kathryn Anne Graystone, which sounded much more the English Shakespearian professional, and no one would suspect her of being Irish, or related to Ryan O'Rourke.

Clair Conner, the youngest of the Conner cousins, was a wee lass herself, only fifteen, who lived in Montana with the McCabes and was not yet old enough to partake in such family business.

Looked as if there was to be a family re-union in Prescott, Arizona.

All were headed that way, except for the Burkes, Lonegan and Brian, second cousins whom the kin only heard from once every ten years, and the McCreeds, also second cousins, who had been in prison more than they'd been out for the past ten years and were still guests of the territory of Montana if Dillon was correct.

Reese smiled, as he knew Dillon had purposefully left Gerrad, Kane, and Killian McCreed out of the equation, even if they were free men by now. Hell, the kin didn't plan to clear out the whole Arizona Territory, and once you got the McCreeds started, they were about as easy to stop as a high tide in Killorglin, from whence the forefathers of the whole bloody Irish bunch had hailed.

Seems a Missouri River boat company had forgotten to pay the McCreeds for a hundred or so cords of wood, and the three McCreeds had helped themselves to a side-wheeler's safe, and only getting three times what was owed them, had put the passengers and crew ashore, then scuttled the boat at a deep trench where only its shiny brass whistle showed above the water.

The McCreeds had never been ones to mess with, and it took a posse of a hundred men, if rumor was correct, to get them into Montana's Deer Lodge Territorial Prison, after shooting each of them full of holes and burning them out of a line shack.

Besides, the McCreed and Burke bunches were only second cousins.

Reese shoved his way through the batwing doors of McGuire's, a little surprised to see the place already busy, the tables full, and the stand-up bar rowdy with drunks. He walked directly to the stairs, elbowing his way through a rough bunch of miners, and mounted them to the office.

He banged once, then opened the door.

Shamus McGuire was at his rolltop desk counting money. He'd snapped up a stubby revolver by the time the door slammed against the wall, leveling it on Reese's middle.

"Reese, damn you, I'm counting last night's receipts."

"Shamus, I've got to be gone a few days, maybe as much as a month."

Shamus signed deeply. "You're my best dealer."

"Remember that as I'll want my job back when I finish this bit of work."

"What's so all-fired important —"

"Kin trouble."

McGuire was silent for a long moment, then shrugged. "I'll do my damnedest to hold your job, but I can't promise. . . ."

"Your damnedest is good enough for me. I'll get back here as quickly as possible."

Reese pulled the door shut behind him.

He heard his boss call out behind him, "Hey, bucko! Don't go gettin' yersef shot fulla holes."

Taking the stairs down two at a time, he again was slowed by the shouldering and elbowing of men.

Just as he reached the batwing doors, he heard his name called out derisively.

"Reese! Reese Conner!"

He knew that voice and tone, and tried to ignore it. It was the same young'un who'd tried to work up his courage the night before.

Ryan had embarrassed the young man by taking his month's wages at the faro table, and it seemed it was coming back to haunt him.

"You getting too damn old to hear, Reese Conner?"

Reese didn't have time for this. He spun on his heel to confront the redheaded young man, who sported a cocked eye. He was four paces away, leaning back against the bar, his hand resting on a chopped-down stubby Army Colt slung low on his hip.

It was an old gun, but old guns had killed many an unwary man.

The saloon suddenly went silent as heads turned, the piano player stopped in mid-tune, and men at the bar backed away from the youth.

But Reese didn't meet the boy's single good eye with his gaze. Instead he glanced around the room, as if he were trying to locate the man who'd called him.

"Conner, I hear you're supposed to be slick as pig shit."

The boy spat on the floor among scattered goober shells. But Reese could discern the quiver in the boy's voice, and he really didn't want to end the kid's sass here in this drunk-filled barroom. There was a chance the kid might come to his senses. His voice raised an octave. "I'll bet you're a yellow back-shootin' son of a bitch!"

He all but yelled the final curse.

Even the sound of breathing halted, as most knew that Reese Conner didn't take insults.

Reese still didn't look him in the eye, but he walked weaving in the boy's direction, purposely limping like a man with a badly gimped leg, glancing around as if he didn't know where he was going. He put a hand to his ear, as if trying to hear.

"Gol'dang, is somebody calling me in that fine alto soprano?"

"You know damn good and well —"

The boy was wide-eyed, his bad eye bulging, as he backed against the bar.

Reese closed the distance in two more limping paces, snaked his own hand out like a rattler, locked a steely grip on the boy's wrist, keeping him from drawing, then clubbed him, *thump!* and *thump!* again, on the side of the head with his heavy Colt, which he'd drawn with the free right hand.

The boy hit the floor like the sack of onions that had rolled off the bar; his eyes rolled up in his head.

The boy had dragged a towel from under the bar as he went down, and knocked over a spittoon, the contents of saliva and tobacco juice staining the floor.

Reese stooped, slipped the boy's stubby revolver out of his holster.

"Ugly damn thing," he muttered.

Flipping the weapon over the bar to the bartender, he then looked back down at the boy.

"Younger, you should never disparage a man's mother, as it's likely to make him angry."

Reese quickly scanned the room; making sure there were no other threats, he holstered his weapon.

He turned back to the bartender. "Howard, hold on to that for a couple of hours. I doubt if this cockeyed Lancelot here will be anxious to get it back, at least not until his headache goes away."

Reese knelt again and touched a spot on the side of the boy's head, his hand coming away bloodied.

"I do believe, however, I split his noggin'. You might want to put a wet bar towel on that."

"My pleasure, Reese," the bartender said with a tight smile.

Scattered nervous laughter rang through the room, the piano player picked up the tune, and men went back to their games.

Again, the exaggerated limp gone, Reese strode to and out the door, then headed for the livery stable where his big gray awaited.

It was a good time to get the hell out of Denver when boys barely shaving decided to call you out.

Ryan dozed the day away, letting sleep heal his bangs and bruises.

He was awakened by the odor of pleasant pipe tobacco, and Dr. Aaron Levy leaning against the bars, calling his name in a low tone.

Ryan sat up, stretched, and winced. "How you doin', Doc?"

"I would be fine if it weren't for talk of hauling you out of this cell and swinging you from a cottonwood outside of town. A lot of talk."

"I left a lot of enemies in Prescott. Every lawman does. But for shootin' some old boy from miles away . . . and only a wound at that. It doesn't make sense."

"The word in the saloons is that you

didn't only shoot this Montez fella, but that you had your way with some old woman who worked there, and with her twelve-year-old granddaughter. That you are a madman, who came out of prison looking for anything to rape and murder. It's getting real mean-sounding out there in the streets."

Nineteen

Aaron's report truly angered Ryan, and he jumped to his feet spitting mad.

"That's a pack of damn lies, Aaron. There was an old woman in that hacienda, but she had a grandson, not a granddaughter. All lies."

"I know that and you know that, but you also know that lies and rumors go through whiskey-soaked saloons like corn through a goose."

"Yeah, and it's my goose that'll get plucked if they get riled enough. Who's doing most of the talking?"

"Some fella named of Boyd seems to be doing most of the stirring. Seems he's somebody in these parts."

"He's somebody all right. A rotten son of a bitch. Owns half the damn town and all the law, and knows what I'll do to him, given time. See what you can do to calm the rabble down, and ask Stinman to step in here if you would."

They talked for a few more minutes;

then, as he left, Aaron asked Stinman to step inside, just as another lawman walked into the office.

Aaron left as both of them walked into the hall separating the six cells.

"You rotten sum'bitch," a familiar voice rang through the bars.

"Well, well," Ryan said, stepping closer to the bars. "If it isn't Deputy Ivan . . . it appears you survived your stroll in the desert."

Ryan could see his white knuckles as the deputy clasped the bars.

"It's Deputy Marshal Metzler to you, you rotten bastard," Metzler growled. "Those other fellas rode out and picked me up. But seein' you behind bars is fine as frog's hair. Only thing better will be seeing you dancin' at the end of a rope."

Ryan was able to muster up a smile, which only made Metzler's knuckles whiten even more.

"By the saints," Ryan said with a coy smile, "that nose of your'n almost healed straight. I swear, you ain't a bit uglier than you was afore I busted it."

Then he ignored the deputy, turning to Stinman. "Hatch, I need to talk with you . . . alone?"

"Hell with you," Metzler snapped. "Anything you got to say to the law, you can say to me."

"Hatch?" Ryan repeated.

Stinman cleared his throat, then turned to the big deputy. "Ivan, he might have something important to say."

"Then tell him to damn well say it."

"Go on . . . step outside. I'll come out in the shake of a lamb's tail and we'll go down the road and have a drink. But step out." Stinman's voice was firm and, sputtering, Metzler did as requested.

"So, what?" Stinman asked, turning back to Ryan.

"I hear there's talk of a lynching?"

"That's just talk, Ryan. Ain't no man gonna come and take one of my prisoners."

"How about a dozen men, or fifty, or a hundred? I hear it's Captain Boyd who's riling them up, and he can do it like nobody else, at least in this town."

Hatcher was quiet for a minute, then shrugged. "I'll tell you what. I'll leave Josh camped out here and the outside doors all locked, just in case somebody tries to sneak in here and do you harm."

"Josh seems like a good man, Hatch, but it'll take more than one if that rabble makes a move on the jail."

"I'm gonna take Metzler down to the saloon and buy him a drink. I'll feel things out and see what the scuttlebutt is. You sit tight," he said, then guffawed.

"I'm glad your sense of humor is working fine. Mine's a mite rusty."

"I'll send Josh in here. It's overtime, you know, to have him stay with you."

"Then take it out of the funds on deposit. By the way, where's Cosgrove? I thought you were gonna have him drop by."

"I haven't seen him lately."

"Well, Hatch, see him." Ryan was beginning to get a little riled. "It could be my hide, so take care of business."

"O'Rourke, I always do. You button your lip and I'll see Cosgrove when I see him."

Ryan was quiet for a moment; then his voice turned hard and cold. "This is no threat or boast, Hatch. If I get lynched, you better go to ordering lumber."

"Why's that, O'Rourke?"

" 'Cause this town won't stand the chance of a snowball in Hades. You'll think Sherman marched through. . . . It'll burn to the ground."

Hatcher drew closer to the bars and glared at Ryan.

"And just how the hell will that happen,

O'Rourke? Lightning bolts from the Good Lord Almighty 'cause you've been such a righteous man all your born days?"

"Enough said, Hatch. Get Cosgrove here to see me, station your man in the hall with a ten-gauge, and for the sake of this whole town calm that lynch mob down. You know damn good and well I didn't lay hands on some old woman or some fledgling of a girl child. That's all bullshit with a capital B."

Ryan turned, walked quietly to his bunk, and flopped down.

Hatcher mumbled as he walked out. "Jesus, Lord, you're an insufferable son of a bitch. Metzler had that right."

In moments, Josh, Hatch's big deputy, walked into the hall, dragging a captain's chair behind him and carrying a newspaper. He sat and propped his legs up on the bars.

"You're gettin' to be a pain, O'Rourke," he mumbled.

Ryan ignored him until, as Josh read, he began to mumble under his breath.

"My God. Oh, no. Sweet Jesus."

"What?" Ryan finally had to ask.

Josh lifted his gaze, and he glared at Ryan.

"You are truly a rotten son of a bitch."

"What are you talking about?"

"Here it is. Right here in the *Gazette.* What you did to that old woman and that little girl."

Ryan leapt to his feet and tried to grab the paper out of Josh's hands, but the big man backed away.

"I'll let you glory in it after I finish."

Ryan walked to the single cell window, and he stood staring out at the alley. Finally, he turned back to Josh.

"You look a mite smarter than that."

"Than what?"

"You believe everything you read?"

"Hell, no, but the *Gazette* —"

"The *Gazette* is controlled by Leander Boyd. If you look behind all the glitter and gold, Leander Boyd is a low-life lying son of a bitch who will meet his maker soon enough, should I get out of this stink hole you call a jail."

"If it's in the *Gazette* . . ." Josh said, and his voice trailed off as he continued to read.

Ryan sighed deeply, flopping back down on the hard bunk. "Don't tarry, kin of mine. Don't tarry," he said under his breath.

Reese was dragging when he plodded into Alamosa after a long, dry two-day ride, most of which was at a fast single-foot across a harsh desert.

He went straight to the little town's only hotel, a single-story affair that couldn't boast more than a half dozen rooms, and stomped up to the desk.

"You got a Garret Conner in here?"

The robust clerk, whose belly showed through the parted buttons on his stained shirt, didn't have to look at the register.

"Why, no, sir, the hotel is empty as a winter hen."

"The stage stop here?"

"It does, over at the livery, once a week, and this afternoon is the day."

"Good. You got two saloons. Which one pours an honest drink of good whiskey?"

"Neither, but the Boston would be your best bet." The man smiled, showing a missing front tooth. "But don't let it be known I was taking sides."

When the stage arrived, Reese was waiting, his dislike of his brother tempered by more than a couple of shots of fine Tennessee sippin' whiskey that the barman poured from a bottle covered with dust.

Garret Conner was a rangy man with salt-and-pepper hair and deep-set, intense eyes.

He unfolded from the stage, a pair of

saddlebags slung over one shoulder, a converted Lemat with holster and belt over the other, his Winchester hanging easily from a rawboned hand. He glared at his little brother, although no longer down at him as they had long been eye to eye.

"Reese," he said simply.

"Ret," Reese replied, and with only a little hesitation, extended his hand.

His brother, acting as if it was some kind of imposition, shook, and as usual it was talon to talon as both of them expended more than necessary energy.

Ret walked to the rear of the stage and recovered a saddle, blanket, and bridle.

"You're missing something," Reese said, a little humor in his voice.

"Oh?"

"The horse."

Ret glared at him, then spat, "Couldn't get here fast enough on horseback."

"I arranged for stock for Ethan and Dillon, but all Dillon said in his wire was to meet you here in two days."

"Two days from Leadville? There isn't a train, Reese, as you damn well know, and no horse could get me here in two days. But never mind, we'll find something. The Good Lord will provide. Let's get at it. It's time to smite those who do Ryan wrong."

Garret had been telling him "never mind" all of their lives, and that "the Good Lord will provide." What it really meant was, "If you can't do it, I will," and it grated Reese's backbone.

He ignored it.

"I met a couple of fellows in the saloon who said they were wranglers. Shall we go have a talk with them?"

"Might'a known you'd found something in a saloon. Let's try the livery."

"It's your butt," Reese said, and decided then and there that this was going to be a long, quiet ride, for he was already through trying to have any kind of a conversation with his brother.

They walked across the road to the livery, where the proprietor was busy changing the Concord's team. They waited, not speaking for a while.

Reese finally gave Garret a condescending smile. "I see you're still toting that old Lemat."

"Yep, and I got another in the bedroll. I'm big enough to tote whatever I damn well please."

Reese shook his head. There was no talking to his brother.

Garret finally asked, "When was the last time you wrote Ma?"

Reese clamped his jaw and said nothing.

"That's what I thought," Garret said, and spat in the dirt.

Reese sighed, and waited.

The hostler finally finished and the stage rattled out.

Reese was a little surprised when his brother shelled out 125 dollars for the hostler's own mount, a tall sorrel with four white stockings and fire in his eyes.

Garret had never been one who enjoyed or appreciated good horseflesh. In fact, he'd normally rather walk than ride.

As Ret saddled the sorrel, Reese couldn't help but note, "You're gonna need a bedroll."

"Don't plan on sleepin' much," Ret said, and swung into the saddle.

In a heartbeat they were pounding west, into the setting sun.

It was just after sundown when the six-up and coach rolled to a creaking stop in front of Prescott's livery and stage station.

Kathleen O'Rourke, professionally known as Kathryn Anne Graystone, with the helping hand of one of the passengers, stepped off the Concord stage and, unladylike — but then actresses were renowned for being unladylike — stretched her arms wide and yawned.

It had been three solid days of bouncing and lurching; eating dust; banging shoulders with other passengers; facing quick lunches and dinners of bacon, beans, and biscuits; and with the exception of one six-hour layover while some harness was repaired, sleeping sitting up in the coach.

She was bone-tired, her body crying for a hot bath, clean sheets, and a feather mattress.

The men could travel in trousers and a loose shirt. Women had to bear up under full skirts, petticoats, high-necked blouses, gloves, button shoes, and by far worst of all, whalebone corsets; and if she didn't get hers off soon, she was going to scream louder than Katherine from *The Taming of the Shrew.*

As usual, every man traveling with her had seen to her smallest whim, but how many whims could be satisfied in a coach jammed with six inside and another half dozen on top, hanging on for dear life?

In addition to twelve men on the coach, all of whom were well armed, they were escorted more than half the way by a squad of six soldiers, who rode thirty to forty miles with the coach, before trading off with another six, to protect it from the Navaho, Pima, and Apache.

Kathleen was about fed up with the company of tobacco-chewing and cigar-smoking rough-hewn men, and having to continue the affectation of being a British snob. She yearned for her leather riding skirt, knee-high doeskin boots, loose blouse, and no bloody whalebone anywhere in the vicinity of her body, unless it was carved into a pipe for a smoke of decent tobacco, but that was not to be, at least not for a few hours.

Her first goal was to establish herself as a lady only concerned with herself, an actress who was interested in a full house and in having her ego fulfilled.

Then she had some serious business to attend to.

Kin business.

Twenty

Almost as soon as she finished the yawn, a tall handsome fellow with wavy dark hair and pork-chop sideburns stepped up and doffed his top hat.

"Miss Graystone, I presume. McManus Peters, manager of the Tempest, at your service. Madam, your posters don't do you justice."

She sighed, ignoring the compliment, too tired to be flattered.

"So you got my wire? I left before I received a reply."

"I did, and we're thrilled to have you here in Prescott."

He eyed the woman, who, even after a long, hard trip in a dusty jouncing wagon, was strikingly beautiful. Her shiny black hair fell to the middle of her back, and her blue eyes sparkled like gemstones.

"Thrilled is wonderful, Mr. Peters, but can you meet my terms and do you have a slot I can fill?"

He smiled and bowed low, sweeping

the hat in an exaggerated motion as he did so.

"If we didn't have one, we would have created one. We have canceled several nights of lectures, but luckily Dr. Cromwell, our scheduled lecturer, has a slight case of the croup and was happy to re-schedule . . . so it's all worked out well. And yes, we can meet your terms, providing you pull at least a three-quarter house."

"Hummm," she said, as if concerned. "Can you fetch my bags? We can talk terms in the morning. If I don't get a hot tub and a feather bed, I'm going to melt."

"My pleasure, madam."

McManus waved at a boy who waited at the boot.

"Get moving, Elias."

The gangly youth, a stagehand at the Tempest, gathered up a large leather trunk and two hatboxes, then yelled out, "Mr. Peters, this trunk is enough for a two-horse team. Can you help with a couple of these?"

McManus ignored the boy; rather he pulled a gold watch from his waistcoat and glanced at the time, at the rest of the passengers, then at the beautiful actress.

"Miss Graystone, I expected you to have a manager or lady-in-waiting in atten-dance?"

"This is a quick trip, and I allowed my traveling companion to go to Denver to see her family. My manager is on his way to California to confirm the importance of some appearances."

"Then I can cancel the smaller room?"

"You may. You do have a suite for me? I believe I'm about to have the vapors."

"Of course, the best in town."

She paused and looked up and down the street, then turned to McManus and decided to investigate in a manner befitting the persona she'd adopted.

"I heard at the last stage stop that you have a hanging in the offing. Will that interfere with the size of the house? I'm not accustomed to a half-empty house."

"Shouldn't interfere. In fact, a hangman's jig" — he smiled, but she didn't return it — "usually fills the town, not that your appearance wouldn't do so. The fact is, we don't have a judge in town, and can't hang the worthless fellow until we do."

"So what did the blackguard do? And who might he be?"

"Rape and attempted murder. A true scoundrel. Another black Irishman gone bad."

"Who, sir?"

"O'Rourke would be his name."

"Never heard of the lout."

"I would be surprised if you had; however, at one time he was a lawman here in Prescott . . . a lawman of some repute. Nonetheless, we'll be fortunate if the miners and drovers hereabout don't take matters into their own hands."

That stopped her short, and she stared at him.

"Just what do you mean, sir?"

"Why, a lynching. No decent man abides by men who mistreat women, particularly little girls."

The heat rose in her cheeks at the thought of her brother being blamed for such a thing, but she calmed herself.

"I would hope not," she said; then fear rolled over her, and the thought of her brother being lynched sent a shudder down her backbone.

But her training as an actress prevailed.

"Thank the Good Lord" — she formed the sign of a prayer, her hands together over her bosom — "that I've never heard tell of him."

Again she sighed deeply, thinking, *Well, hanging Ryan seems a foregone conclusion, but at least not a fulfilled wish. I'm in time. Now if the rest of the kin would only get here.* She willed herself to look appalled.

"I don't abide by hanging, mind you, but then I certainly don't abide the mistreatment of ladies. In fact, as Shakespeare observed, 'many a good hanging prevents a bad marriage.' So this affair might possibly protect some poor soul of the weaker sex who might fall for his charms."

She smiled and batted her eyes again.

"Oh, well, sir, life goes on. If you would be so kind, my bath and bed?"

"Soon, madam. Your wish is my command. But please" — he flashed her his most charming smile — "please indulge us. Mr. Boyd, who owns the Tempest, and Mr. Vaca, a prominent ranchero, and his ward . . . a lovely young lady about your age . . . would be honored if you'd join us all for a late supper in the hotel dining room. I'm sure you're famished."

She smiled, but shook her head.

"Actually, I'm too tired to eat, and in no frame of mind to be sociable. Would a late breakfast do? A very, very late breakfast?"

"If you insist."

"I do, sir. I absolutely, positively, indubitably insist."

"Then tomorrow . . . say eleven?"

"Say one, and please, good East India tea, champagne, Scotch eggs, and biscuits light enough to float away. Oh, yes, and strawberries with clotted cream . . . if you would be so kind."

"I'll do my very best."

She batted her eyes as she reached up and patted him on a smooth-shaven cheek. He must have visited the barber late in the day in honor of her arrival.

"McManus, I'm sure your best would please even Queen Victoria." Her elocution was in her best British accent.

As McManus escorted her to the Palace, he couldn't help but think, *Where the hell am I going to get champagne? And who in town knows how to make Scotch eggs, or clotted cream for that matter? Actresses, a pain in the ass. But this one, renowned for her soliloquies and singing, and her obvious beauty, should fill the house and make us all a pocket full of gold. So kissing her pretty backside for a few days will be worth it. In fact, kissing her anywhere for any reason would be a pleasure.*

McManus frowned at the boy, but walked over and picked up another hatbox and a valise. The selection of her bags among many was easy, as all were leather, a polished mahogany color, with gleaming brass buckles.

She did relent to at least be introduced to Mr. Boyd, Señor Vaca, and his ward, Felicia, as they passed. And she was surprised to see that the don's ward was a beautiful Anglo girl.

Kathleen eyed her carefully, now angry that she'd agreed to be introduced before she was rested and had redone her makeup.

This Felicia McCall was a beautiful woman, and the fact McManus thought them the same age testified to how tired and haggard she was, as the woman was years older, probably Ryan's age. Kathleen felt the heat on her cheeks. Now all of them would think her no more than a tired old hag.

The men were both handsome and mannerly, but were more than likely scoundrels. They were men of means, and seldom do men acquire means if they're not something of the rascal and blackguard.

She'd ferret all that out soon enough.

Rather than don her nightgown, after her bath she pulled on her split leather riding skirt and a dark, long-sleeved blouse, leaving her boots until later, and lay on top of the bed.

She carried a watch, a gold French-made repeater, twice the depth of the normal pocket watch, that she'd carefully packed as it was very expensive. It had an alarm that could be set, and when the winder was pushed down it rang not only the hour, but the quarter hour and the minute. It had kept her on time for many an appearance.

She set it for three a.m., and in moments fell into an exhausted sleep.

Aluishious Cosgrove stared bleary-eyed through the bars. "So, whash the crime, O'Rourke?"

"I'm told I'm to be tried for attempted murder and rape, although it's all bunk."

"Always ish." Cosgrove laughed.

"Al, I'm telling you. I shot a man who'd already pulled a gun on me, and I never touched Vaca's women."

"Well, Ron —"

"It's Ryan, Al. You remember me. Ryan O'Rourke. I used to be a deputy marshal right here in Prescott."

"Yep. Thas what I said, Ryan. We can file us a writ of habeas corpus, kind of a 'produce the body' thing, on this . . . to produce the victims . . . and insist that the man who you is . . . are . . . accused of shootin' holes in is here to testify, as the women you raped should be as well, although the court is not inclined to make those kind of victims show up."

"There aren't women, only one woman, and she's old as Methuselah. And I didn't rape anyone. She had her grandson there —"

"Jesus J. Christ . . . you raped a boy?"

Ryan glared at the drunken lawyer. "Al, come back in the morning when you're sober."

He started to turn away, then turned back, almost falling as he did so. "Sir, there is the masser . . . the matter . . . of a retainer."

"In the morning, Cosgrove. You think you can remember to come back in the morning?"

"Of course, sir. I am an officer of the court, a courtly man . . . a man who has read the law. I will return." He waved a finger, then tipped a beat-up top hat and turned to the door, again almost tripping.

"Early, Cosgrove, before you've had a drink, and I'll have a retainer waiting."

"I do not partake of demon rum, sir."

After Aluishious Cosgrove stumbled out the door, Ryan walked over and flopped on his bunk. *Jesus J. Christ is right,* he thought, *I'm at the mercy of fools. I've got to break out of here, if kin doesn't show up soon.*

Nico Vaca, Felicia McCall, and Leander Boyd sat in the hotel dining room, finishing off their meal with brandies, and in the case of the men, cigars.

"So," Nico said, "it appears that Señor Tobar did not agree to appoint a judge?"

"No, he flat-out refused," Boyd said, sipping his brandy, then laughed. "And he threatened all hell to pay should I speak of the Slovakian lady in my employ. He's a man of principle . . . but I'm working on another solution."

"I've heard talk of a lynching."

"It'll be more than talk come tomorrow night. I've got my boys ready to hooray the crowd in both our saloons. They'll have pockets fulla money to buy drinks, and I've rehearsed them all as to what to say. I'll more than likely speak myself. We'll stir up the crowd enough that they'll go after Ryan with a roar and a rope."

"And Marshal Stinman?" Vaca asked.

"He's my man, at least mostly. He gets things in his craw once in a while, so I arranged for him to have to go to Phoenix, but he'll be back inside a week."

"Bueno," Vaca said.

"Gentlemen . . . I think you're both disgusting," Felicia said, rising to her feet, her voice ringing with derision. "I believe it's time for me to retire."

Boyd laughed. "You opposed to hanging, lass?"

"No, I'm not. But I'm opposed to murder, and that's what you're stirring up."

Nico reddened. "Yes, *querida,* it is time for you to retire. Do so, now. I'll be up shortly."

"Nico, as far as I'm concerned, you can sit here all night and drink yourself into a stupor."

"*Buenas noches,* Felicia," he said, his tone cold and a little ominous.

She turned and headed to the lobby and stairway.

Lee Boyd laughed and slapped his thigh.

"My God, man, that's a sassy woman. I do believe she has you buffaloed and befuddled."

"You know, *mi amigo,*" Nico said, his tone low and ominous, "your brandy is excellent, and your dinner was even better, but your mouth will get you into terrible trouble someday."

Boyd's eyes narrowed, and his massive

shoulders hunkered forward. "You better run along upstairs, Vaca, before your lady friend packs up and heads out for parts unknown."

Nico jerked to his feet, knocking the brandy over as he did so.

"You've had too much to drink, Señor."

"Not so much as I plan to have. Then I'll head over to the Sundown and keep the talk going, and keep solving your problems and mine."

"You do that, run your mouth to others more tolerant. I am retiring."

"I believe it is time to call it a night, partner," Lee Boyd said, his tone sarcastic.

They parted ways.

As Lee Boyd watched his partner walk away, he wondered. If something happened to Nico Vaca, whom would the woman take up with? She was incredibly beautiful and desirable, and he'd always wanted her. Knowing her as he'd come to, he knew that most likely she'd follow the largest poke of gold, and after Nico Vaca, that was him, Lee Boyd.

And, of course, there was the matter of the ownership of the saloons and brothels. All of them were moneymakers, and he now split the money with Vaca.

All of Vaca's relations were far away

down near the border, and if Vaca went to meet his maker, Lee should be able to easily buy out the heirs' interest, and if it came to using the law to do so, the law in Prescott favored Anglos, and besides, Lee Boyd owned most of the law in town.

If Vaca wasn't around, there was the woman, and even more money.

Lee downed the last of his brandy and decided to head for the Sundown, his saloon, and Nico Vaca's, of course.

At least for a while.

It was something to think on.

Twenty-one

Kathleen had to fight to get her eyes open when she realized she wasn't dreaming, and heard the repeater's few notes of the old song "Greensleaves" signaling three a.m.

But she managed to pry weary lids open, sat on the edge of the big bed, pulled on her boots, and got to her feet. She stuffed a full head of middle-of-the-back-length black hair into a wide floppy-brimmed drover's hat, and took a deep breath. Hopefully, with the dark clothes and hat she wouldn't be noticed on the street — if there was anyone on the street.

Quietly she slipped out of the door to the suite and tiptoed down the hall to the back stairway.

She waited in the shadows of the alley until the street seemed completely quiet, then moved quickly across and over the boardwalk on the other side, working her way alongside the mercantile store until she found a back alley.

Almost exactly a block down the alley,

crossing a side street to get there, she came to the single-story stone building that was the territorial marshal's office and jail.

Kathleen was only a little over five feet tall, and the sill of the windows was five feet off the ground. There were four windows on this side of the building, three small ones in the rear, spaced as if they might be cells, and a larger one near the front. The smaller ones were shuttered, and closed and padlocked from the outside at night to keep anyone from passing a firearm through to an occupant.

The jail backed up to a barn. She moved back and across the alley to a hay yard behind the barn and found a bucket. Then back to the windows. At each of the first two she listened for some time at the crack between the padlocked shutters — padlocked at dark every night — and heard nothing. At the third, she discerned the sounds of a man sleeping heavily, snoring lightly, occasionally sputtering.

"Ryan," she whispered, then again more loudly, "Ryan!"

"Mama," she heard a drunken unfamiliar voice call out.

She remained silent as a man sputtered in an inebriated sleep, his breathing evening out again.

She dismounted, picked the bucket up, and circled the jail to the far side. It too had three smaller windows and a larger one nearer the street.

At the first window, she again heard a man's heavy breathing. She noticed a knot in the shutter and cracked it with the heel of her palm, and it popped out.

"Ryan," she again whispered through the hole, then more loudly, "Ryan! Wake up!"

But the breathing continued. She climbed down from the bucket and searched the dirt walkway separating the jail from the building next door, until she found a handful of small stones.

This time after she called his name, she flipped a pebble through the hole at the sound of his breathing. After the third call and flip, she heard someone turn over and feet padding toward the window. But she kept her eye glued to the hole.

A face appeared in the starlight, and at first she didn't recognize the bearded man with eyes cut and swollen.

"By the saints," he said, and no one could mistake that deep baritone. "As I live and breathe, if it ain't me little sis."

"I'm balanced on a bucket here, bucko. Tell me in one breath what's going on."

And in one breath, he told her of his trouble with Nico Vaca and Lee Boyd, and that they were setting him up to be strung up.

"Then we have to get you out of here."

"Where's the rest of those louts you call cousins?"

"On their way, God willin'. Anything I can have brought to you?" she asked, already feeling she was pressing her luck with her time at the window.

"A few sticks of dynamite and a fast horse," he said, then laughed.

"Glad you can still make a smile, bucko. I'm gone. I'm short on sleep and I wouldn't be surprised if I'm going to be needing to be well rested."

"I'd toast you if I had a dram," he said, sticking his index finger through the knothole.

She hooked his index finger with hers. "Here's to absent friends, and to enemies soon to be absent from God's green earth," she said, then released his finger and disappeared.

He called after her, "Katy, me love, there's a woman, Felicia McCall . . . see what's on her mind, you have a chance."

"Right, me bucko. I'll try and come back tomorrow night with that dram," he heard her voice call back; then she was gone.

He was smiling when he went back to sleep.

When the deputy, Josh, brought Ryan his morning coffee and a bowl of mush, Josh informed him he had a visitor. Ryan expected the lawyer Al Cosgrove, and was surprised, and almost pleased, to see he was mistaken.

His recently renewed friendship was confirmed when a big sombrero over an ample body filled the doorway from the office. Innocente Alverez Robles, who had fed him on the trail, ambled over to the bars.

"*Amigo,* they treat you well?"

Ryan slipped a hand through the bars and shook. "Well enough, as jails go."

"I have brought you something," Innocente said, fishing in a cloth sack he carried, then coming up with a couple of tortillas. One was wrapped around chunks of pork and peppers, the other filled with chocolate.

"You are a gentleman, Innocente," Ryan said with a grin.

"I had a bottle of *pulque,* but they took it from me," the big man said, shrugging.

"They get their pound of flesh. So, did your proposition for the sale of horses work out?" Ryan asked, his mouth full.

"*Sí, señor.* I will deliver fifty head at forty dollars each. I will drive one hundred head to the fort, and the hostler will have his choice of the lot. We leave tomorrow for Fort Verde."

"And Leander Boyd?"

"So far, I have not heard from Señor Boyd."

Ryan frowned. "Watch him, he's a snake. He has ears everywhere. Don't count on him not knowing."

"It is time this snake is stepped upon; however, as with the serpent, it is best to avoid him if one can. If one cannot, then one must cut the head off."

They visited for a while; then Innocente took his leave. He had a long ride to his rancho, then another long drive back to Fort Verde.

As soon as the big man left, Ryan yelled for Josh. "Damn, Deputy, can you bring me some water?" The peppers were taking their toll.

McManus Peters wasted no time taking advantage of his unexpected boon, the arrival of Kathryn Anne Graystone. He in-

264

formed her at their late breakfast that he had four musicians ready for an afternoon rehearsal, and her first performance scheduled for the following night.

"That's fine, McManus," she said.

The men, Nico Vaca and Leander Boyd, had monopolized her, but when Nico finally turned his attention to Lee Boyd, she was able to engage the other lady in conversation.

"And where are you from, Miss McCall?" Kathleen asked.

"Chicago originally, but I've been here in Prescott for some time."

"And you enjoy it?"

Felicia smiled tightly. "I did, but it's a hard place. Full of hard men with rough manners."

"Señor Vaca seems the gentleman," Kathleen said, prying.

"Of course, or I wouldn't have allowed him to become a friend and protector. But, of course, he's a *haciendado,* and they have special ways."

"When we have some time, I'd love to talk more."

"It would be my pleasure," Felicia said.

Kathleen stared out the window of the hotel dining room for a moment, then turned her attention back to Felicia. "Do you know this man who's the subject of so much talk?"

"Who?"

"O'Rourke, I believe they say."

"Yes, I know Ryan O'Rourke well. I fear for him."

"Oh. You know him that well?"

"We were . . . were friends when he was a deputy marshal here." She bowed her head, feigning distress. "At least until he shot and killed my betrothed."

"My God," Kathleen said, also acting. "What was the circumstance?"

"There was a disagreement over business. Mr. O'Rourke went to prison for the shooting, but only for a short time. There was some question of self-defense."

She overheard the men talking, heads together, thinking they could not be heard, and Lee Boyd said, "Tonight should be the night. They'll drag him out . . . ."

"Interesting," Kathleen said, as if she were responding to Felicia. Then the women's conversation was interrupted as Lee Boyd turned his attention back to them. She desperately thought of what she might do to delay anything happening until her kin arrived. Then she thought of a plan. . . .

"So, ladies," Lee asked, "have you had

your fill? I'm sure Miss Graystone would like to get to the Tempest to rehearse."

Kathleen smiled, her tone condescending. "Thank you, Mr. Boyd, but actually, I'm far more concerned about the musicians . . . and the size of the house."

"I assure you, madam," McManus interrupted, "our gentlemen are top quality, and we'll get the word out."

"Shall we see how good your locals are?" Kathleen said, rising from the table.

As the men bowed, and as if an afterthought, Kathleen turned to Lee Boyd. "Mr. Boyd, I occasionally enjoy the bawdiness of a saloon crowd, as they're so appreciative, and it helps build the house, particularly when we haven't had time for posters. Would your saloon, I believe it's called the Sundown, would your patrons enjoy my appearance for a song or two?" She knew the answer before she asked.

Boyd's face lit up, then fell again. "And this would be included in what you're already being paid?"

"I'm sorry, but that's crass, sir. I don't discuss money, but if I did, I'd tell you that I work very hard to make sure I have a full house, to satisfy everyone involved. It would be my pleasure to appear, for the good of all."

He beamed. "I'm sorry to be so direct, Miss Graystone, but business is business. What time?"

"Say, nine o'clock?"

"Perfect, we'll make sure your Tempest musicians are available."

"Thank you, but the piano will suffice."

"You're sure?"

"Of course."

"Then tonight."

Kathleen turned to Felicia. "I miss the company of my own, Miss McCall. Would you consider coming to the opera house this afternoon, to enjoy tea and cake with me?"

"At four?"

"Teatime, you know our British customs. Four would be perfect."

Kathleen turned to McManus. "Will you see to it, sir?"

"Of course, ladies."

After McManus escorted her out, and Felicia excused herself to her room, Vaca zeroed his eyes in on his partner. "That was foolish, Señor. It will interfere with your plan to ignite this lynching. She is a beautiful woman, who I understand sings like the very angels, and no man will leave the saloon during her presence."

Boyd was so interested in the money

Kathryn Anne Graystone would generate for the coffers of the saloon, he'd forgotten about the night's plan.

"Ah, hell," Boyd groused, "we'll still make it happen. I figured on ten or so, but it'll be later. The house will be packed when I get the word out, more fuel for our fire. Besides, she'll make us an easy five or six hundred more than usual."

"I hope you are correct. I want to see this matter with Señor O'Rourke end. It is time I returned to Rancho Conejo."

Boyd shrugged, then laughed before he offered, "You going home won't break my heart, partner. But *pasa tiempo,* Nico. Ain't that what you rancheros say, that there ain't no hurry — *pasa tiempo?*"

"Stay with your English, Señor. You have enough trouble with it."

Nico headed for the door, and left without a good-bye.

"You pompous ass," Boyd snarled after he'd left the dining room. "Speaking of time, your time has about come," he mumbled at the empty doorway, but his partner was long gone.

Twenty-two

Kathryn Anne Graystone, known to her family as Kathleen O'Rourke, entered the Sundown on Leander Boyd's arm, and the place, standing room only, hushed and men jerked off hats and parted as he escorted her to the elevated stage at the rear of the place where a piano rested.

The piano player, Anthony Azevido, a heavyset man as bald as a billiard ball, wearing black trousers, a white shirt with billowing sleeves, a black top hat, and a red garter on his shirt sleeve, stopped playing as she approached.

He even resigned himself to dropping his cigar in the spittoon at the side of his bench.

Nico Vaca and Felicia McCall, with whom Kathryn had enjoyed tea and cake a few hours before, were seated at Boyd's normal table on the balcony.

At Kathryn's request, the Sundown was prepared to lower the chandeliers and re-duce the lighting from four oil lamps on each fixture to one. Only the lights lining the foot of the stage, each with a polished reflector, would remain fully lit.

By the time she reached the stage, the lights had lowered by their ropes and three of each four lamps put out, the others lowered to dim.

The piano player had spent most of the afternoon at the Tempest, working on the arrangements she wanted. For a man with fat stubby hands and fingers, he played well enough to suit her.

The piano player rose and bowed deeply as Leander escorted Kathryn on stage. It was silent as a tomb as Lee Boyd cleared his throat and introduced her.

"The Sundown is pleased and honored to introduce the talented and internationally known Miss Kathryn Anne Graystone, here all the way from old England, to entertain us with a song or two . . . I hope more."

The applause began, but Lee quieted them, then continued.

"Miss Graystone has sung for Queen Vic and Prime Minister Benjamin Disraeli; at the Theatre Royal, Covent Garden, and Drury Lane" — he had to glance at the notes she had given him, then read on — "for Emperor Franz Joseph and his court, and for King Umberto of Italy.

"She's appeared at all the great music halls of America. She will begin her three-night run at the Tempest tomorrow night, and I expect you all to be there, particularly after taking advantage of her kindness and enjoying this entertainment.

"Tickets are on sale at the box office, at Suzzette's Saloon, or here at the bar."

"Thank you, Leander," Kathryn said, and curtsied to the crowd, who broke into raucous applause and cheers.

She nodded to the piano player, who struck some introductory notes, and as quickly as the crowd had grown noisy, they became dead still.

Her voice was as clear and pure as a crisp December morning, warm and soothing as a cup of hot chocolate, and surprisingly powerful.

She began with two popular Stephen Foster songs, "Old Folks at Home" — commonly called "Suwannee River" — and "Beautiful Dreamer," which almost brought the house down, then a hymn, "Swing Low, Sweet Chariot," then "Ave Maria," which brought several of the men to tears.

She then sang "Father, Dear Father, Come Home with Me Now," a temperance song that made Leander wince and the men stop drinking, but only momentarily.

Finally, she ended with a stirring rendition of the "Star-Spangled Banner."

Hats that hadn't been removed, now were.

They thought they were about to get another song, but they weren't. She quieted the applause, then addressed them.

"Gentlemen, and I know in my heart of hearts you are that . . . gentlemen . . . however, there is talk of lynching a man, hanging him without benefit of trial."

She continued, as if she were from Britain, and not as American as any there.

"Those of you who believe in that great song I just completed, and in this great country, know that to be an act not worthy of your America, which you've all fought so hard to preserve . . . for which so many have recently died during the great war of rebellion."

She hung her head as if in sorrow, then looked up, and scanned the room with her piercing blue eyes, meeting as many eyes as possible.

"I hope, I pray, that you won't sink to the bestial depths of such depravity. As God is my witness, I think I would never be able to sing again if I witnessed such a heinous act."

There was dead silence in the room.

She made a great show of removing her handkerchief and wiping her eyes.

"Would you like another song?" she asked, sniffling as she did.

The house roared.

"I would love to sing for you, but you must promise me this man, no matter how low he has sunk, will get a fair trial. A trial worthy of this great country."

Still, there was silence.

"Promise me! With a cheer that he can hear all the way over at the jail."

The place swelled with the shouts.

She quieted them, then sang three more stirring songs. When she bowed at their completion, the crowd stomped the floor, almost rocking the place, until she agreed to sing "Ave Maria" again.

When she hurried off the stage, she was surprised to come face-to-face with Cousin Reese and Cousin Garret, dark circles under their eyes, still dusty from the trail.

She whispered her room number and hotel as she passed, and they nodded, then elbowed their way to the bar.

As Lee Boyd escorted Kathryn up the stairs to join them, Nico Vaca, incensed, turned to his tablemate. "Felicia, *mi amor,* while you enjoyed your tea and cake, did you convince Miss Graystone to give that oration regarding Señor Ryan O'Rourke?"

"Why, no, Nico. The subject of Mr. O'Rourke never came up. We talked only of lady things."

His eyes narrowed. "I think you lie, *querida*."

"And I think, *querido,* if you call me a liar again, you'll be drinking . . . and sleeping . . . without my company."

She could see the muscles in his jaw knot, before he spoke in a harsh whisper.

"Felicia, your company does not mean life or death to me, but mine might . . . to you."

"Is that a threat?" she asked, her eyes sparking, but he wasn't able to answer; he rose to his feet as Lee Boyd and Kathryn Graystone approached.

Nico turned his attention to Kathryn Graystone. "Señorita Graystone, your singing was inspired by the angels." Then his tone hardened. "I had no idea you are such a pacifist."

"A pacifist, sir?"

"*Sí,* your plea to keep Señor O'Rourke from being hanged by this angry town."

"It has nothing to do with pacifism, kind sir. It has to do with the law. The West is lawless enough without a whole town par-taking in crime."

Nico smiled tightly. "So, do you have some kind of ax to grind regarding this particular criminal?"

"Why, sir, I couldn't tell you his name if my life depended on it." It was one of her best performances.

Again, Nico smiled, eying her carefully. "So, you came to Prescott so suddenly for what reason?"

Lee Boyd interrupted. "My God, Nico, you sound like a prosecutor . . . it's not Miss Graystone who's awaiting trial."

Nico snapped, glaring at Lee, "Nothing can interfere . . ."

He didn't complete the accusation as it would inform Miss Graystone of much too much; instead he turned back to her and ignored Boyd.

"For what reason?" he repeated.

Kathryn reached up and patted Lee Boyd's cheek as if he were a three-year-old.

"It's all right, Mr. Boyd."

She turned back to Nico.

"I came here, sir, as I've never been here, and heard it was beautiful, if rugged, country. I had a rest period, some free time, and didn't feel the need of resting. And I hoped for a nice opera house, and

Mr. Boyd" — she batted her eyes at Lee — "has one of the nicest in the West."

"Even so," Nico pressed, "Prescott seems a strange place for such a world traveler to be interested in visiting."

"Why," Kathryn said with a little too much fervor and finality, "I find it pleasant, and what a nice audience." She had a touch of ice in her voice as she continued. "So, is the judge and jury satisfied?"

She didn't wait for or expect an answer; rather she turned to Felicia.

"Don't you think so, Miss McCall . . . that Prescott's a wonderful place with wonderful people?"

"Why, yes, *most* everyone here in Prescott is pleasant." Felicia's tone rang with sarcasm, and she eyed Nico as if he were something stuck on the sole of her high-buttoned shoe, until he glared back at her and she cut her eyes away.

Kathryn turned to Lee.

"Mr. Boyd, I'd appreciate it if you'd escort me back to my room, if you'll all excuse me. I still haven't fully recovered from the trip."

It was after midnight, as she lay awake, again dressed in her riding skirt and doeskin boots, when she heard a soft knock on her door.

In moments, Kathleen, Reese, and Garret were outside Ryan's cell window and she had her brother awake and engaged in the conversation he'd long been awaiting.

After the greetings, Garret commented, "Ry, we've come a long way to get you shook loose of this problem. You going to head for Montana, we get you out?"

Ryan was silent for a moment, considering his answer. "It's not that easy, Ret. There are four men right here in Prescott that shamed me and took a good part of my life from me. That's got to be dealt with."

Reese nodded in agreement, but Garret was not satisfied.

"So, we should risk getting you out of here and having you get thrown right back inside, and maybe us too."

Even through the board shutters, you could hear the anger and determination in Ryan's voice.

"Garret, if the kin so wants, they can all turn around and go right back where y'all came from. And you have my appreciation for comin'. As for me, I've got to do what I have to do."

Reese spoke up. "And that's your decision, and it's ours to be here. We'll get you out; then you do what you have to, and if you want my help, you've damn sure got it."

Garret spoke before Ryan could.

"We'll get you out, Ry; then we'll talk again and see if you come to your senses. The Good Lord will have his own way with those who've lied and cheated their way through life."

Again there was silence, before Ryan said, "Maybe, Ret, but not quickly enough to suit me. The Lord helps those who help themselves."

For the first time, Kathleen spoke up.

"Dillon and young Ethan should arrive tomorrow or the next day, God willin'. It might be wise to wait until we've got all the help possible . . . presuming that mob doesn't get riled again."

Reese laughed, giving Kathleen a hug with an arm around her shoulder. "I think you did a job on the mob." Then he turned to the crack in the shutters. "Those ol' boys is all in love with little Kathleen, and if she asked them to head to the North Pole in their nakeds, they'd go off with hat in hand and nothing else."

"We'll be back tomorrow night," Garret said to the crack in the shutters, then turned to the other two. "Let's get out of here before some drunk stumbles along and we have to smite him like a bug."

Reese leaned close. "You hold on, Ry, we'll be back."

"Y'all watch out for a couple of fellas besides Lee Boyd and Nico Vaca. Filo Parkinson and Henry Holstadt were on that jury that railroaded me, and they were both lickin' Lee Boyd's hand, and putting the heavy hand on the good folks in the chairs next to them, the whole time. And they were members of the so-called vigilante committee that started all this trouble and that all the good folks fear.

"And be on the lookout for a vaquero, Innocente Robles . . . big fella, and a friend. He let me know that Boyd has been on the prod, and has hired at least six shooters. He'll back your play, as he's got his own bone to pick with Boyd and Vaca.

"And another fella, Dr. Aaron Levy, a fine old man, a snake-oil peddler and jack-of-all-trades, who's been a real friend."

"We'll keep our eyes peeled," Reese said, and they left.

Ryan hadn't seen Levy in a couple of days, but the old man had mentioned working the surrounding mines, farms, and ranches. Ryan was sure he'd see him again soon, if the kin could get Ryan out of jail or at least keep the mob at bay.

While the kin spoke, another meeting was under way in the Sundown.

Extra chairs had been brought to circle Lee Boyd's table on the balcony, where his six hired men — including Parkinson and Holstadt — and two of Nico Vaca's vaqueros, lieutenants, waited as Boyd and Vaca gave them all instructions.

"We won't get as many of the towns-people as I'd hoped," Boyd said, "since Miss Graystone gave her little talk, but we'll get enough."

"So," Parkinson asked, "when do you want this all to happen?" Parkinson was tall and thin, his head almost touching doorjambs when he passed through. He wore a black holster with silver conchos, a nickel-plated revolver over his city suit, and a bowler hat. He looked like a lawyer turned gunfighter for the moment.

Holstadt was short and broad, with the affectation of wearing the fanciest of em-broidered waistcoats, but had gained weight and they wouldn't button. He wore them nonetheless. His favorite companion was a sawed-off double-barrel express guard's gun. He'd worked as an express guard for many years. His bowler hat was pushed low enough that it flattened his ears, one of which was cauliflowered from someone's well-earned hard left hook.

Lee Boyd glanced at Nico before he answered. "Tomorrow night?" He got a nod from Nico, so he continued. "With the Rancho Conejo vaqueros, over twenty men, and with our six, we've got the main bunch, maybe enough, to storm the jail and drag O'Rourke out of there. It's time this son of a bitch paid the piper."

After the others had left, Nico eyed Boyd and spoke to him as if he were a subordinate. "Leander, you will see that this happens. It is a thorn in my side, one that you must remove if you wish to remain in my good graces."

Lee Boyd snarled, "Nico, I don't much give a damn about your good graces. But the fact is, Hatch will be back from Phoenix in a couple of days, and I don't want him around when the jail is rushed."

"If you were doing your job, Boyd, he would be firmly in our camp and would be no problem. Make this end, *amigo,* or I will."

"And that means?" Boyd almost rested a hand on his revolver, but restrained himself. It was neither the time nor the place.

"It means . . . exactly . . . what I said."

Nico rose and strode away, giving Lee Boyd his back.

I'm gonna have to kill that pompous son of a bitch, Boyd thought, watching him go. *And I'm going to relish it.*

Twenty-three

Kathleen awoke and went through her usual routine when she faced a performance.

After her ablutions, she dressed and took a pleasant walk up and down the main street, stopping in the mercantile and viewing Prescott's latest in female accoutrements — parasols and gloves — of which there was a very limited offering, those on hand being two years out of fashion.

Then she returned to the hotel, where an invitation awaited for the Ladies Botanical Society annual meeting, scheduled for that afternoon. She sent a note, politely declining, explaining that she must rest her voice. After a leisurely, if late, breakfast of two soft-boiled eggs and a glass of warm milk, she returned to her room, placed a warm wet towel over her eyes, and did, in fact, rest her voice. After a while, she removed the towel and read sheet music, going over lyrics.

Garret and Reese Conner, on the other hand, stayed busy, if you could call staying quiet and mostly listening staying busy. They worked apart so their association would not be common knowledge, went to separate restaurants for both breakfast and lunch, and went to the tonsorial parlor for a shave at different times to pick up the local gossip.

They'd scheduled a meeting on a bench in front of the territorial government building at five p.m., and did join up there, each of them having a smoke, Garret with a small carved meerschaum pipe and Reese rolling the makings. Garret carried a *Gazette* tucked under his arm. Each of them basically ignored the other, but they talked under their breath.

"So, you learn anything?" Garret asked.

"The same everywhere," Reese said. "This O'Rourke fella is the scum of the earth and doesn't deserve to live. I'd be surprised if we have time to wait for Ethan and Dillon if they don't ride in by tonight. This town is boiling over, no matter how good a job Kathleen did at quieting things down."

Garret shook his head ruefully before he replied. "I tried to find this Innocente fella that Ry mentioned, but heard he'd left town."

"And I've kept my eyes open for the snake-oil salesman, but no sign of a wagon or Dr. Levy."

"Anything else?" Garret asked, rising, his back to Reese.

"Nope, maybe we'll learn more in the pubs."

"You ought to take a look at this," Garret said. "I hope to hell it isn't true, 'cause if it is, the Good Lord is not on our side." He dropped the newspaper on the bench. "I'm going to take another look at that jail and see what field of fire is offered by the surroundings. You line up a good horse for Ryan. I'll be in the Sundown and in Suzzette's tonight."

Then he strode away.

Reese could feel the heat rise on the back of his neck and his veins bulge as he read the long article in the *Gazette*. Unlike Garret, he knew damn well the article was all lies. In fact, he noted the names of the publisher and editor on the masthead, hoping that he might run into them so he could shove one of their sharp quill pens where the sun didn't shine.

He wadded the paper into a ball and dropped it under the bench, then looked up to see a brightly painted wagon, pulled by a matching set of mules wearing tassels on their harness, turn off the dirt lane from the west onto the brick street of Prescott.

He sat back down, deciding to let the wagon come to him.

When it came even, he stepped off the boardwalk and walked to meet it. The man driving was old, but dressed well and sporting a fine white Vandyke beard, and he had a quickness of eye and manner to him.

"You Dr. Levy?" Reese asked.

The man looked him up and down, then offered, "Nobody else in this wagon, and that's what the sign on the side says."

"Got a moment to jaw?"

The doctor smiled. "You got some ailments need attention? If so, I got a tonic that'll have you kickin' up your heels and howling at the moon."

"I'll bet. I got several aches and pains, but that's not the subject. Ry is."

"Ry?"

"Ryan O'Rourke."

"Gee," he yelled at the mules. "Let me tie this team."

They had to set up chairs gathered from the saloons in the Tempest in addition to the 125 permanent seats, and men were packed out into the lobby, looking through the two sets of doors leading into the main theater.

Four boxes, each normally accommodating eight patrons, lined the walls well above the common seats, and each of them was filled with twelve of the town's elite, including Arnold Tobar, acting governor in Fremont's absence.

As a result, the saloons were sparse of clientele, with not even one of the faro tables full of players. Ret leaned against the bar of Suzzette's, talking with a townsman who obviously was not an aficionado of fine music. The saloon connected to one of Boyd's brothels by a short hallway, and several of the girls loitered around a table near the hallway. Ret discouraged one working girl who'd walked over and greeted him.

"The Lord loves Jezebels as well as honest, hard-working, God-fearing souls, but I got no money for you, darling.

"You'd spend your time better in search of a husband or honest work."

The girl was obviously seeking neither a sermon nor advice; she scowled at Garret as she hurried away.

Even the piano was silent as the musician had refused to miss Kathryn Anne Graystone's performance.

Ret hadn't finished his beer when Reese walked in and sidled up next to him.

Reese tipped his hat at the bartender.

"Irish whiskey, if you got the real stuff."

"I do," the runny-eyed rotund barman said, wiping the bar with a towel, "but the real stuff is a half-dollar a shot, and it won't be an overly generous one."

"Better a small taste of the best than a bath in the normal swill."

The bartender moved away, fetching a stool to reach a bottle well up on a shelf.

Under his breath, Reese said, "Dr. Aaron Levy is waiting for us round back at the Spotted Horse. Come on down there when you can get out of here."

Garret merely gave his brother a slight nod. He'd seen the sign on the livery at the edge of town, and knew where they'd be.

Reese upended the shot glass, paid, and walked out.

Garret took his time, finally sucking the last of the foam out of the beer, and followed.

They met in the darkness behind the livery, leaning against Levy's wagon. "So, Dr. Levy," Garret said after he'd been introduced, "do you know Ryan well?"

Dr. Levy was working a deep-bowed pipe, so Garret packed and lit his meerschaum.

Levy exhaled a long cloud of tobacco smoke. "Well enough to believe him innocent of what's he been accused."

"So you don't condone this talk going around?"

Levy studied the tall man before he responded, then cleared his throat. "Mr. Conner, I come from a people who've been persecuted for centuries. I don't condone wrong, no matter what its form."

"Then you'll consider doing the Christian thing . . . helping us?" Garret asked.

Reese spoke up before Levy could answer. "It might be dangerous. I passed twenty-five vaqueros down the block a ways, standing around talking and drinking *pulque.* I don't figure them to be planning a fiesta as there wasn't a señorita to be seen."

Levy smiled sadly. "I'm a God-fearing man of the Jewish faith, Mr. Conner. If doing what's right is the Christian thing, then it's mine to do as well." He eyed them both in turn. "Gentlemen, you think an old man traveling alone in this wild land doesn't know danger? I hate firearms, and I hate killing, but I hate the thought of hateful crowds even more, particularly of men seeking vengeance when none is due.

"Killing begets killing, but it's been my sad experience to learn that turning the other cheek is no real solution.

"I'll help, but I won't pick up a gun . . . unless a grievous wrong will result from my not."

"No need," Garret said. "We do right fine in the firearm department."

Then, as an afterthought, Garret asked, "But you have a firearm?"

"I do, a fine Sharps rifle as a matter of fact, as I love the occasional antelope, and a double-barrel express gun with brass shells, the plain ones with shot to fill my larder with quail, grouse, and the occasional duck, goose, or turkey, and ones marked with an X scratch and loaded with cut-up horseshoe nails. I have those for my use, as well as a half dozen other firearms for sale."

Garret smiled. "And the ones loaded with nails are for?"

"Varmints," he said, but his look said Indians and bandits.

Smiling, Garret turned to Reese and, as usual, his smile faded.

"Did you find a sound horse?"

"Several, but none I'd trust to outrun a posse."

"For Ryan obviously?" Aaron Levy asked. Garret nodded.

"Then," Levy said with a shake of his head, "you don't plan to wait for a trial?"

Reese shrugged. "Don't think this town will let him get to trial, and if he did, the jury would be as loaded as those X shells of your'n."

"Then there's no need for another horse. He's got a fine dun gelding, well rested, right here in this livery, as well as a decent little mule. That dun horse already outran half the country, and has proved up to any task.

"I'm sure Boyd, who owns this place, figures on running up a feed bill and owning them, as well as Ryan's gear, which is stowed in a cabinet inside. Saddle, bridle, a Smith and Wesson Russian that I sold him, a brand new Winchester he bought in Yuma, and his bedroll and personals."

"Problem solved," Reese said.

They talked a while longer, investigated the wagon, then worked out a plan that allowed Dr. Levy to stay as remote as possible, yet still be of help, and parted ways.

Reese pulled Garret aside as Levy plodded away.

"I think we should bust him out right now, before Kathleen's show breaks up, while half the town is in the theater."

"No. I don't want posters out on me. I've never had to look over my shoulder, and I'm not about to start now. And I want to wait until Dillon and Ethan show up. If lead has to fly, I want Dillon's fine hand. I don't plan a nimbus around my head."

Reese sighed. "What the hell's a nimbus?"

"That's the gentle glow that surrounds the faces of all of God's good angels. I'm not ready to meet my maker yet. We wait."

"Don't count on endin' up being an angel." He couldn't help but guffaw, then added, "Better posters than a dead kinsman."

"No posters. We wait."

"Easy as pie right now," Reese pressed, but he knew his older brother and how hardheaded he could be. He'd made up his mind, and a pry bar couldn't change it, particularly if the suggestion of change came from Reese.

"Easy? Nothing's easy. Posters on all three of us sure as hell isn't easy!" Garret snapped. "No! We wait. I'll shoot down every mother's sinning son if it has to be done. But we wait until it *has* to be done, one way or the other." Then his voice hardened even more. "One thing is for sure, as sure as there's a God in heaven, no one is going to hang one of the kin. Not while another still lives."

"And when the hell did you see an angel?" Reese said with a slight snarl in his voice.

Garret merely glared at him.

Reese knotted his jaw, but said nothing more.

"Ryan, you are a troublesome sort," Josh, the big deputy, said. "Me missing this big show don't make me like you more'n a low-down coyote. How-some-ever, you can help make up for it if you'll lose a few hands of cribbage."

Ryan yawned and stretched his arms, then agreed. "Sorry you can't make the concert. I hear she's got the voice of the Archangel, and is pretty as a new calf. You got a cribbage board?"

"Would I suggest cribbage if'n I didn't?" He disappeared out the hallway door and was gone for a long time, then finally returned with a deck and board.

"I about fell off to sleep," Ryan said. "What kept you so long?"

"Some fella looking for a deputy marshal's job stopped by to chew the fat. Too damn good-lookin' and fancied up to be a deputy, though."

"Oh. He have a name?"

"Conners, I think he said."

"From down on the border?" Ryan asked, knowing damn well where he was from. He smiled with some relief.

"Believe he said he was here fresh from Texas."

Now Ryan smiled wryly. "If Hatch is looking for help, I'm a fair hand."

"Ha."

"You gonna deal or gab?"

Josh had pulled an extra chair up to the bars to use for a table.

After they'd played the first game, Ryan asked, "You got a loaded scattergun lying nearby?"

"In the other room, and no, you can't borrow it."

"I don't suppose you'd consider fetching it, and locking that middle door."

Josh eyed him dubiously. "And why would I do that?"

" 'Cause a couple of vaqueros have paused at my window and checked things out twice now . . . and I don't think they're looking for accommodations in this fine establishment."

Josh glanced at the window. "You deal,

and don't cheat. I'm gonna fetch a few things and see what's going on outside while we still got a touch of light. I should get the padlocks on those shutters anyhow."

"Josh," Ryan said, his tone insistent, "I'd sure think you oughta bring the scattergun, and a full box of ammo for that Remington Frontier, when you come on back."

Josh nodded, patting the big Remington revolver he wore.

Ryan went to the window, but no one was in sight.

With one of the Conners coming to call, probably Reese, as Josh had described how he was dressed, and a couple of strange vaqueros reconnoitering the alley, something was damn sure up.

Things could get interesting in a big hurry.

Twenty-four

The concert ended promptly at ten p.m., and the saloons began filling up. Kathleen was a little surprised, and suspicious, that she hadn't been invited to a late supper by Boyd and Vaca. She'd seen them, together with Miss McCall, in the prime box near the stage front.

But no one other than the normal admirers had appeared backstage.

It was just as well, as she had business that needed attention.

The young stagehand, Elias, who'd unloaded her luggage, escorted her back to her hotel room, and she quickly changed clothes.

As agreed, Reese and Garret Conner were armed and in positions scouted out earlier in the day.

Reese had found an excellent vantage point in a tall white building only three doors down from the jail. A building with a three-story spire that looked out over all but the hotel and was eye to eye with the highest floor there.

He figured the Good Lord wouldn't mind if he borrowed the bell tower of the Lutheran church to get the angle on the front of the jail, and even part of the alley behind.

He'd had to jimmy a window, as the stairway up to the bell began inside, even though the bell rope hung into a cubical open to the street. The bell doubled as a call to emergency for fires or other matters, saving the volunteer fire department the trouble and expense of building their own.

He mounted the stairs carrying not only his rifle and two Lemats, but a canvas sack with boxes of ammo and other items he'd picked up at the mercantile earlier in the day.

Items he figured might be put to good use, should this night end in violence. He did not intend to be on the short end of that stick.

Garret was directly across the brick street on the roof, behind the false front of the mercantile. He was not as high as Reese, but he could see not only the front of the jail, but a good ways down both side yards.

They'd agreed to stay in those protective positions until the town was quiet for the night, which more than likely would not be until after three a.m.

Both of them had more than two boxes of .44/40 shells for their Winchesters, and a belt of revolver cartridges. Reese wore a Colt on his hip, and Garret a pair of heavy Lemats. The Lemats each had nine shots in a revolving cylinder, with a converted .44 barrel fitted to center-fire cartridges, plus a unique twenty-gauge shotgun barrel below it. With the flip of the alignment of the striker on the hammer, the weapon would discharge the upper or lower barrel. They were formidable weapons, well suited to infighting.

If anyone stormed the jail this night, they'd pay dearly.

Twenty-five

Waiting until the Sundown was full with men returning from the concert, and with the piano again tinkling out a lively tune, Leander Boyd downed a shot of fine Irish whiskey, rose from the balcony table he again shared with Felicia McCall and Nico Vaca, and walked to the railing.

If Filo Parkinson was following instructions, he was doing the same thing in Suzzette's, at the edge of town, with an even more low-life and excitable crowd, and with Henry Holstadt in the midst of that crowd cheering them on and jeering at the thought of Ryan O'Rourke still being alive in "their town."

He stooped so he could see Swartzy, the bartender, serving drinks as fast as he could pour them, and called down. "Swartzy, tell Azivedo to kill that racket."

Swartz rounded the end of the bar and mounted the stage to yell at the piano player, "Anthony, the boss says knock it off."

When the playing abruptly stopped, all heads turned to the stage, and when Boyd yelled out, all eyes were raised to the balcony.

"Gentlemen, I hope you enjoyed the concert tonight." A cheer arose. "I think we should talk of something more serious than entertainment. You all know I have a vested interest in the future of Prescott." He paused to acknowledge the agreement and nodding of heads. "And you all know that I believe in law and order." The head-nodding was somewhat less pronounced with that declaration. "We have a man in our jail who committed the most heinous of crimes, the rape of a wonderful old grandmother, and far worse than even that travesty, her grandchild, deflowered in her most innocent years. Is this the kind of man we want in our town?"

Booing shook the place.

"I know most of you well, and I agree. A man like Ryan O'Rourke doesn't deserve to live among decent folk . . . in fact, doesn't deserve to live at all. It's just too bad we don't have a judge here so we can get on with hanging him. I guess Judge Coleman thought visiting with those high-binders in the East more important than ridding your town, Prescott, of this scum.

He thinks more of the ladies of Washington than he does of your own, right here. I guess it's up to you to protect your women and children."

He waited for the vocal agreement to fade, then smiled at the crowd. "I so appreciate your feelings about this despicable son of a whore and the rumors of action that I hear. Of course, all they are so far is rumors. And rumors, gentlemen, won't keep your women and children safe. Only action will do that."

The cheers and jeers again arose.

"In fact, I'm going to show you how much I appreciate it." He checked his pocket watch, then again bent far over the rail and shouted down. "Swartzy, drinks are on the house for one hour."

This time the cheers literally shook the building.

Felicia rose from her chair. "I think I'm going to the hotel. I've had enough of you two for one night." She rose and strode away.

"Faint heart?" Boyd asked Vaca with a snide smile.

Vaca snarled, "I am beginning to believe that she lacks something between the ears, as she does not know what is good for her."

Boyd laughed. "Why don't you send her back to town if you think she is so ignorant?"

Vaca narrowed his eyes. "And you would like that, her having no protector?"

"Don't mean spit to me, Vaca," Boyd said, smiling too much.

Vaca smiled tightly. "Intelligence is not all I find interesting in a woman. In fact, it is of little importance."

Boyd decided now was as good a time as any to give Vaca a last chance. "Nico, how about selling me your interest in the saloons and the brothels? And since you seem to detest this woman, why don't you leave her here . . . in my care?"

Nico snapped, "You will see the sun rise in the west first, *amigo*."

"Stranger things have happened, *amigo*. Stranger things."

Nico rose and turned to walk away, then turned back suddenly. "Leander, I have two thousand dollars in my room. You begin drawing a bill of sale for both the saloons and the brothels, and I will buy you out."

"Ha," Boyd said, and spat into the cuspidor at his side. He glowered at Vaca. "That wouldn't buy the Sundown, much less all of them."

"Three thousand?" Vaca snapped.

"The hell with you, Nico."

"My last offer, *amigo*."

"A wise man would ride out of here, back to his rancho."

Vaca's eyes narrowed. "Tomorrow, Leander. Tomorrow I have made arrangements for John McFadden from the bank to begin auditing the books of all of our joint holdings. I presume that is no problem?"

"That's your right, Nico," Boyd said, but his voice rang hollow, and he looked very distant.

Nico again gave Boyd his back, stalking away, descending the stairs, and leaving the saloon. He went straight to the hotel, took those stairs two at a time all the way to the third floor, and reached a hand out to throw Felicia's door open, but found it locked. He rattled it and got no response. Glancing down the hall, he saw the door to Kathryn Graystone's suite open, but just momentarily. Someone in a leather skirt and floppy-brimmed hat had glanced out, then quickly shut the door. Not the kind of dress he would expect a stage celebrity to wear. He wondered who it might be, but had more important things on his mind.

He entered his room, slamming the door

behind him, and walked straight to the connecting door with Felicia's room, and found it too locked.

"*Querida,* open the door," he demanded.

He got no response, so he pounded on it with the flat of his hand.

"Felicia, open the damned door, or I will kick it in."

Hearing movement in the room, he waited patiently, until he heard the latch slide away. "It's open," he heard Felicia say.

He stomped inside as she, dressed in a nightgown with a wrap tightly and modestly tied around her, returned to her bed. Without removing the wrap, she climbed under the covers.

"I'm tired, Nico."

As usual, he felt the heat in his loins, and his tone changed, softened.

"I want to give you something, angel . . . a peace offering."

"Oh," she said, seemingly disinterested.

"Come into my room."

"I'm tired, Nico."

His voice hardened slightly. "You said that already, *querida.* You are tired far too often of late. My peace offering might make you less tired."

She yawned, but climbed from the bed

and followed him, padding across the room in her bare feet. He went to his leather valise and flipped open the top, then reached in and removed a small metal box. Fishing in his waistcoat pocket, he removed a key.

He smiled at her, but she still gave him a cold, disinterested look.

"When this business is concluded, little angel, I would like to take you to Mexico City."

Again, she yawned, so he opened the little box, and her eyes grew wider and much more interested.

"You do like gold, do you not, my sweet angel?"

This garnered a small smile and a warm glance. "Doesn't everyone, Nico?"

"I believe that everyone does." He carefully began to count, until he reached twenty-five, and handed her the heaping handful of twenty-dollar gold pieces. "This is five hundred dollars, little angel. This is for you. When we get to Mexico City, some of the finest seamstresses in the world will make you two dozen dresses, with matching parasols and reticules, for this amount of money. Ladies who were trained in Paris, and who are the best in the world at what they do."

She glanced at him doubtfully, but moved the coins from one hand to the other, seemingly loving the feel of the cold coins in her hand.

This time, her smile was dazzling. "Nico, you are a handsome and generous man."

"Then close the door and come to my bed for the night."

"Of course, Nico." She reached up with her free hand and caressed his cheek, as she batted her eyes. She started to turn away, then said, "Nico. *Querido.* How much coin do you carry in that little box?"

"There is another twenty-five hundred or so there, little angel. But of course, that is a very small portion of what I have . . . but you knew that. I merely grabbed a couple of handfuls before we left the rancho, where I have a safe as large as the bank's . . . full of coin and script."

"Of course," she said, and crossed the room to close the door, thinking, *But it's enough to get me to St. Louis in style, and to keep me in style, until I find another man, an even richer man, and maybe, just maybe, this time, one whom I can stomach.*

As she returned from turning down her lamps and closing the connecting door, he was already undressed and patting the bed beside where he lay. His serpent smile almost sickened her, but she came on.

"Little angel," he said, almost as an afterthought, "put the coins back in the box, and I will hold them for safekeeping, until we return to the rancho."

"Of course, Nico, for safekeeping." *You bastard,* she thought. *I can't wait to get out of this town, and away from you and Leander Boyd.*

But with the three thousand, of course.

She returned the coins, checking the remaining ones to confirm what he'd said. Yes, there could be three thousand there total. Enough. She smiled joyously, almost skipping to join him.

He too smiled, but not at her returning to his bed, at the thought that, after tonight, there would be no more Ryan O'Rourke to cloud her judgment . . . if that was what had seemed to preoccupy her thoughts of late.

And just possibly, no more Leander Boyd to interfere with his plans.

Twenty-six

Kathleen had stepped back inside her room when she realized Nico Vaca was in the hallway. She had to move past his room to get to the back stairway and out of the hotel into the alley. She'd waited until he entered the room and closed the door tightly behind himself.

It was good that the split leather riding skirt she wore had deep pockets, for it was thus easy to conceal the .32-caliber Hopkins and Allen pocket revolver.

The little gun would also fit in her reticule, and she had carried it many times when leaving a theater late at night, pulling and cocking it more than one time to discourage an overeager admirer, or a stalker with even more evil intentions.

The perils of being on stage.

Garret had been waiting just inside the back stairway door earlier when she'd left for the theater, and had instructed her to meet Dr. Levy in the alleyway behind the livery stable after the show, and she was headed there.

He had also given her strict instructions to stay away if trouble started.

As if she would.

She had almost reached the bottom landing when she heard a distant gunshot. She stopped dead still, listening, then heard the raucous sounds of men in the street.

She hurried out the back door and down the side yard to where she could see a group of men, forty or more, marching down the street, coming from the direction of Suzzette's, heading toward the jail.

She'd have no time to join Dr. Levy.

A couple more gunshots were fired in the air, and she heard, "O'Rourke!" shouted more than once.

Instead of heading for the livery, she fell in twenty paces behind the moving crowd, staying on the boardwalk.

When they'd traveled another half block, one of the men leading the group broke and ran for the doors of the Sundown.

Boyd was on the balcony inside, enjoying the growing discontent of the crowd below as they drank his free whiskey, when Henry Holstadt flung open the batwing doors of the saloon and shouted, "Any of you who's man enough, come on. We're gonna hang that bastard O'Rourke." He backed out and hurried to join the passing gang.

Voices were raised in the saloon, but no one moved toward the door.

Boyd shouted until the room quieted. "Gentlemen, drinking time has ended until O'Rourke swings. But for those of you who do the Lord's good work tonight, there'll be another hour on the house when you return."

The crowd upended glasses and mugs, then surged toward the swinging doors.

Boyd couldn't contain himself, but he began to guffaw, and was still laughing as he descended the stairs to fall in behind.

Josh, the deputy, was up, scattergun in one hand, padlock in the other, barring and locking the door connecting the cells to the office. At the sound of the first shot he'd thrown his cards aside and run to the office to clean out the rifle and ammunition racks.

"You gonna give me a rifle, Josh?" Ryan asked.

"Hell, no. We don't know that's not just a bunch of drovers hoorayin' being in town."

"There may be drovers among them. I knotted the head of enough of them when

I had your job, and they may carry a grudge. But there are paid guns as well."

"You just sit tight. Damn, I wish Hatch was here."

"I don't," Ryan said. "Hatch is Boyd's man —"

"The hell he is," Josh snapped. "Keep your mouth shut so's I can hear what's going on out there."

"Don't take no high-tone professor to figure out what's going on. Boyd's men, and probably Vaca's men too, are coming to lynch me up."

"You probably deserve it," Josh said. "Now shut up."

There was a small opening in the connecting door, with bars, but it wouldn't prevent a pistol or rifle barrel being shoved through.

The sounds of men shouting and shooting drew nearer.

But before the crowds reached the jail, Josh heard the pounding of hooves up to the front of the jail, and then boots slamming against the plank boardwalk. He'd locked the front door of the jail also, and heard the door rattle.

Then two gunshots blew the lock and knob all to hell, and the door was shoved open.

Josh jammed the barrels of the scatter-gun through the bars in the little opening, and shouted, "Stay the hell out of here, or I'll fill your belly with lead."

Two men had appeared in the doorway, but disappeared just as quickly.

Then shouts rang out. "We're here to help. That's our kin you've got in there. It's Ethan and Dillon McCabe."

Josh turned to Ryan. "You got kin named McCabe?"

"I do. Couple of ugly louts with eyes like slake ice. Let them in."

"Hell, they may be worse than that crowd."

Ryan managed a tight grin. "Likely they are, but they won't do you harm, and they'll sure as hell do me some good, God willin'."

"Well, this does seem to be gettin' somewhat out of hand." They could hear the crowd sounds almost reaching the jail.

"How about it?" the voice from the outside doorway yelled again.

"Okay, come on in, but you've got to stay in the office."

Two men burst through the doorway and slammed it behind them. One of them ran to Hatch Stinman's chair, dragged it across the floor, and propped it hard under the knob.

He wouldn't have done that, Josh surmised, had he not been wanting to keep the crowd out.

At least he had some help. Of course, it was help that probably wanted O'Rourke out of his jail as much as did the crowd, albeit for another reason.

He might just be out of the skillet and into the fire.

Felicia McCall was sleeping heavily, even with the sounds of gunfire in the street.

Vaca, hearing the sounds of the passing crowd, arose and quickly dressed. This was not something he wanted to miss. O'Rourke had been a stone in his boot long enough, and he would not only see him hang, but see that he had more than one hole in his chest after he was strung up. The man had proved to be like the gata, the cat, and to have more than one life. Besides, if things got wild and more shots flew, there were other things he might accomplish.

He grabbed a Winchester from where it leaned in a corner of the room, slipped out the door, and ran to the back stairway. He did not wish to be associated with this lynching, but he wanted to make sure it happened, and he worried that Boyd would foul up the attempt again.

Keeping to the alley, Vaca ran until he was even with the jail, then worked his way down a side yard until he could see the men gathering in front of the territorial jailhouse. Many men. At least a hundred, including his vaqueros.

They were tearing down the hitching rail in front of the jail. He wondered for a moment what good tearing down the hitching rail could possibly be, then got the answer. A half dozen of them mounted the boardwalk, spaced themselves along the rail, and began using it as a battering ram.

He smiled. This would be over soon; then he could deal with Leander Boyd, and all of his problems would be solved.

"Poco tiempo," he told himself. *"Poco tiempo."* Ten feet from the boardwalk, unseen from the street, he leaned back against the building to watch. Then he smiled as Leander Boyd passed. Vaca moved closer to the street so he could watch Boyd, but stayed in the shadows out of sight.

Reese Conner was atop the very building against which Nico Vaca leaned, but could not see him from his perch behind the false front.

Reese was about to scatter the crowd

below, when a shot rang out from the bell tower of the church. Garret. The man in the front of the battering ram, a man who had been pointed out to him earlier as Henry Holstadt, collapsed in a heap in front of the jailhouse door, grabbing his upper thigh and screaming.

As the others stared at Holstadt, wondering what had happened, Reese centered his Winchester's sight on the second man. His rifle bucked and the second man spun away, then began crawling down the boardwalk. If his aim was true, the doctor would be busy setting broken legs.

Firing erupted from inside the jail, as two rifles appeared through slots in the closed and locked shutters.

Reese had seen Ethan and Dillon arrive, and smiled as they'd blown their way into the jailhouse. He knew that the men forming up outside were about to get the surprise of their lives, had they gotten through the door.

Men began to run for cover, as they realized what was happening, that their temporary comrades were falling to gunfire. A few of them, unknowing, ran toward the church.

Men gathering below the steeple was just what Garret hoped for. He had spent a good part of the last ten years of his life working in the mines, and prospecting, and he well knew the power of his afternoon purchase.

He fished a stick of dynamite out of the canvas sack he'd lugged up the stairway, shoved a detonator and its twelve-inch fuse in the end of the stick, pulled a lucifer across the striker on the matchbox, and lit the fuse — not on its end but only an inch and a half from the stick — then began counting.

He let it burn halfway, then smiled and lofted it down into the street below. Before it hit the street, it exploded.

Men began to scream and scatter.

By the time he could prepare another, he had no target, except for two men dragging a wounded comrade across the street, and that was hardly a sporting target. And, of course, he'd learned well when fighting in the recent unpleasantness, as his mother had called the war before she'd gone on to her reward, that a wounded man was much more trouble for the enemy than a dead one.

Meanwhile, Josh yelled at the two men in the front office, "What's happening out there?"

"Well," Dillon said, "besides a hundred

317

men wanting our hides, gunfire, and dynamite going off in the street, not much."

"That was dynamite?" Josh asked.

There was a pause before Dillon answered. "What the hell do you think it was, the world's by God biggest Fourth of July Chinese firecracker?"

Josh moved back from the connecting door, his scattergun in one hand, his .44/40 Remington Frontier in the other. "This is more than I bargained for," he said to no one in particular. "They could blow us up like kindling."

Then he backed almost against the bars of Ryan's cell.

Ryan looped a powerful arm around Josh's neck, at the same time wrenching the Remington out of his hand.

"Drop the scattergun, Josh," Ryan said, his voice low and soothing, even if the arm cutting off Josh's breath wasn't. The scattergun clattered to the floor.

"Damn you, O'Rourke," the deputy said when Ryan released him.

"Now fish those keys out and open up."

He did as told.

Ryan smiled at him. "I'm gonna lock you up in here, but not for long, as I'm afraid they might get the roof to burning and it would fall in on you. And I don't want to lose a cribbage pardner. You unlock this door and back away."

"You'd let me go?" Josh asked, wide-eyed, as he worked the cell door lock.

"Not if you don't get on with it. I got things to do . . . kin to say howdy to that I haven't seen in a long time . . . and a bunch of townfolk to deal with."

Josh swung the cell door aside. As Ryan locked him in the cell, Josh shouted and shook his fist. "Ain't gonna be no more cribbage."

"It's your turn to keep quiet, Josh. I'll let you go as soon as I'm sure you won't get shot down running out the back door, which would sure as hell be laid on me."

Ryan moved to the connecting door and unlocked it. "Coming out, y'all."

He moved through the door, carrying Josh's scattergun and Remington.

"Howdy," he said to his two cousins. Both the McCabes were as tall as Ryan, if thinner, and both had striking blue eyes and coal-black hair. They were easily recognized.

"Why, howdy, Cousin Ry," young Ethan said, "fancy seeing you here."

"I'd rather be fishin' the Yellowstone," Dillon said. "Ain't it about time we headed out that way?" Just as he finished the sentence, gunfire began to splatter the shutters and door.

All of them dove to the floor.

"Could be we waited a mite too long," Dillon said. "How about the back door?" he asked Ryan.

"Hell, those old boys in the street scattered every which way. Let's give it a minute to see if Reese and Garret scatter them a little more."

"Reese and Garret here?" Ethan asked.

"Yep, and so's my little sis."

"Well, I'll be damn," Dillon said. "We all ought to sashay down to the saloon and tip us a few for old times."

"How about in Denver?" Ethan said, then ducked even lower as a new volley of cartridges holed the shutters and door.

"Damn you, you're gonna kill me dead," a panicked voice rang out from just outside the jail door.

Ryan looked puzzled for a minute. He moved over against the stone wall, next to the door, and listened for a minute.

"Who's out there?" he yelled.

"It's Henry. Henry Holstadt. Damn, Josh, let me in. These asses don't care who they kill."

Ryan smiled and rose to stand next to the door, still sheltered by the stone. He moved the chair away, and Henry Holstadt fell through onto the floor.

He immediately reached down and grasped his upper leg, not even looking up to see who was his benefactor. Ryan bent and snaked the man's revolver out of his holster.

"What the hell . . ." Holstadt managed. Then he moaned as his eyes focused on Ryan. "Damn the flies."

"You'll damn more than that before this day is over," Ryan said.

"Bind up this leg," Holstadt begged. "I'm gonna bleed to death."

Ethan moved over beside the man, pulling his neckerchief off as he did.

"Hold up," Ryan demanded. "This is one of the lowlifes who got me sent away."

"That was Boyd," Holstadt pleaded. "Bind this afore I bleed out."

Ethan again reached, but Ryan put a hand on his shoulder, stopping him.

"To the back, Henry," Ryan said.

"Then will you patch me up?" Henry asked.

"Soon as you tell Josh what happened in that jury room, I'll bind you up."

Almost before he could finish the sentence, with more lead shattering the shutters and front door, Holstadt was crawling on his hands and one knee to the cell block, dragging his broken leg.

He got inside the connecting door and began spilling everything he knew to Josh. Ryan unlocked the door and let Holstadt crawl inside the cell.

"You said you was letting me go," Josh said.

"I am, soon as it's safe. And soon as you hear Henry out and get him to write it down and put his mark on it."

"About what?" Josh asked.

"About Lee Boyd and Nico Vaca, and fixing that jury that railroaded me, and settin' up this lynching . . . that right, Henry?"

"Fix my damn leg," Holstadt whimpered.

Josh shrugged. Ryan crabbed back into the office and fetched the writing implements and paper, and returned, shoving them and the handkerchief through the bars.

"Don't fix it until he writes it out," Ryan said, but Josh immediately began binding the man's leg.

"Henry, I'll cut the damn thing off, you don't write the truth," Ryan told him. "You understand?"

The man nodded weakly.

In the steeple and behind the false front,

Garret and Reese had begun their deadly work. A half dozen more men had fallen to wounds before they realized the men on the roof and in the steeple were not friends. Only then did bullets begin to peck at their locations. Both the Conner boys kept their heads down and worked on their next move.

Nico Vaca stayed in the shadows, and was not surprised when three men ducked into the side yard where he stayed well hidden.

And to his great pleasure, one of them was Leander Boyd. From the hands of the gods.

In moments, Boyd had instructed one of the men, who slipped out of the side yard and moved away out of sight. The other, whom Vaca knew to be Filo Parkinson, stood next to Boyd, locked in quiet but seemingly insistent conversation.

This was the chance Nico had waited for, and what a perfect situation. Two problems could be solved at one time.

He raised the Winchester, and with gunshots ringing up and down the street, shot Leander Boyd right between the shoulder blades. He slammed forward into the dirt face-first.

Parkinson spun in surprise, reaching for

his sidearm, but Vaca already had the Winchester levered and centered on his chest.

"Do not draw, *amigo,* or you die like Boyd."

"You gonna kill me?" Parkinson asked.

"Possibly. I need a man to manage the saloons and the brothels. A man who is faithful and respectful. Is that man you?"

"Why, sure, Mr. Vaca. What does this job pay?"

Nico smiled. "One, I do not kill you where you stand. Two, you tell how a stray shot killed Boyd. And three, seventy-five dollars a month to start, then more if the businesses become more profitable."

"Why, Mr. Vaca, you got yourself a manager."

"And bodyguard. I know of your reputation with those *pistolas*. And it is *Señor* Vaca, not mister."

"Yes, sir, *Señor* Vaca."

"Your first job is to make sure O'Rourke hangs this night, and that will bring you your first bonus."

"Yes, sir. We'll get the bastard."

"Come to the hotel when it is over."

Vaca slipped away to the rear alley and disappeared.

Parkinson moved to the front of the side yard and began firing at the jailhouse.

He had no idea what hit him when Reese Conner, having heard all that had transpired, slipped off the rooftop and brought his Winchester across Parkinson's head as he hit the ground.

Parkinson went down hard, beside the man who'd been his former boss.

A half block away, a couple more sticks of dynamite exploded in the street, sending men scampering.

Reese smiled. Garret might be obstinate and ornery, and worthless as a brother, but he was useful in a fight, and always had been. Reese had often had the knots to prove it.

Just as Reese was about to break across the street to the jailhouse, before the chunks of soil from the explosions had all landed, he was surprised to hear the pounding of what must be a hundred horses coming.

Was the rabble charging the jailhouse, like Jeb Stuart at the battle of First Manassas at Bull Run?

Then he was surprised to note that the horses were without riders and were being driven by three vaqueros. The rabble were scattering in front of the pounding hooves, breaking from cover behind water troughs and hitching rails, and running for all their lives to escape what appeared to be a stampede.

Reese was even more surprised to see one of the vaqueros slide to a stop in front of the jailhouse and fly from the saddle.

He was a big man, but surprisingly light on his feet. Reese brought him into his sights as the man hit the door, only to find it locked or barred. Even over the pounding of horse hooves and the occasional gunshot, Reese could hear him yelling, "Señor O'Rourke, it is Innocente, let me in."

Reese let his muzzle drop. This was the man Ryan had mentioned, Innocente Robles. Reese too broke for the jailhouse, arriving just as did Garret. The big Mexican swung and reached for his weapon, but both Garret and Reese held their hands up, palms out, and yelled, "Friends. *Amigos.* Ryan's kin." They ran up beside him, their muzzles pointed at the ground.

All of them burst through the doorway, ending up on the jailhouse floor as the door was slammed behind them.

All the other men in the room were also on the floor. One of them smiled and extended a hand to Innocente. "Ethan McCabe, Señor. You're a friend of Ryan's here?"

"Sí, señor."

"Well," Ethan said with a grin, "any friend of this hooligan is a friend of the McCabes."

As soon as Innocente had finished a hard handshake with Ethan, another of the men stuck out his hand.

"And the Conners. That fellow with the big grin" — Garret had his usual dour face on — "is Garret, and I'm Reese. Pleased to meet you."

Ryan sidled up beside Innocente and put a hand on the big man's shoulder. "Thank you for that little stampede."

Innocente grinned and shrugged. "I came to town to see how you were getting along, and Señor Levy told me that some problems might be heading your way." He shrugged again. "I do not know how that happened, Señor. The horses, they just run away down Main Street. It is unfortunate."

"Right," Ryan said, then turned to the others. "Now that all of you are inside here with me, how the hell are we gonna get out?"

Reese shrugged, then said, "That fella Boyd was shot down by the other one, Vaca. Boyd is dead over in the side yard across the street. Vaca told that Parkinson fella that he would meet him back at the hotel."

"And Parkinson?" Ryan asked.

"I clubbed him down with my rifle butt. A little on the hard side maybe."

"Damn hard, I hope."

"The old boy may not wake up."

"There weren't but a couple of them in the back alley," Garret said, "from what I could see. Let's saunter out that way and head for the livery where we got our horses holed up."

Ryan crabbed over to the connecting door. "Josh, you got that paper finished?"

"I do, and it's mighty interesting."

"You got Holstadt bound up so he don't bleed out? Not that I much give a damn."

"I do, and I don't believe he's gonna die."

"Too damn bad," Ryan said, and moved over to the bars. "Give me the paper."

Josh passed it through and Ryan folded it and stuffed it into his shirt pocket. "I signed it as a witness, Ryan. I hope that was okay?"

"You bet. It looks like those fools haven't figured on burning the roof, and I believe you're safer right here than on the street."

"The hell —" Josh began, but Ryan stopped him.

"Here, with the cell unlocked. We're

gonna get the hell out of here, and if I was you, I'd sit tight."

Ryan opened the cell door as he talked, while the others joined him in the cell block hallway.

"How about my Remington?" Josh asked.

Ryan opened the Remington and let the cartridges drop to the floor, then slid the weapon into one of the other cells and locked its door. "The keys will be out there in the alley when you get around to looking for them. You can tell Hatch a half dozen of us jumped you, and I'll back you up."

Josh shrugged. The others had gathered around the back door. Strangely, the firing had stopped.

"What's up?" Ryan asked.

"The hell if I know," Reese said, but moved back into the office and found a spot where he could see at least a part of the street through a bullet hole.

Then he heard why the shooting had stopped, as the sound of a man playing a violin and a beautiful voice rang up and down the streets of Prescott.

The old man and his snake-oil wagon were parked in front of the jailhouse. He sat on the wagon seat, a violin in hand, bowing it with great intensity, and

Kathleen, known as Kathryn Anne Graystone to the rabble, stood on the seat, singing "Ave Maria" with a clarity that would quiet even the songbirds.

The only life in the street other than men peeking from hiding places was a few horses, riderless, standing quietly in the street and drinking from horse troughs. Even the horses finally raised their heads to listen.

Slowly, men began to filter out of the side yards and from where they'd taken shelter in doorways. Some of them limped badly, leaning on their friends. A couple of men were being carried.

When the song ended, Kathleen raised her hands. "Gentlemen, enough is enough. Take your wounded to the doctor and go home to your wives. Prescott is shamed enough for one night."

Reese walked to the shutters and opened them, standing in the darkness of the jail office, watching as men began to move away, while others gathered around the wagon. "Sing it again," they shouted. The old man smiled and began to play, as Kathleen gladly repeated the song.

Reese turned to the others. "It looks like Kathleen has them wrapped around her finger again. Let's get the hell out of here."

Carefully, they moved to the back door and into the alley, then sprinted away toward the livery.

When they reached there, the horses were where they'd been left, saddled and tied to a hitching rail at the rear.

"Anyone for Denver?" Ethan asked, mounting.

"I got a couple more pieces of business," Ryan said, swinging into the saddle of the dun.

"What now?" Garret snapped.

"Nico Vaca, and I got a woman I need to have a minute with."

"Jesus," Garret mumbled in an uncharacteristic curse. "What the hell —"

"You want me to go with you?" Reese asked.

"Thanks, Reese, but this is something I have to do myself. I'll catch up with y'all."

"We'll wait in Alamosa," Garret said, "if you don't catch up with us before." The rest of them nodded their agreement. Then Garret added, "I'm damn tired of this, so don't get put back in the hoosegow."

Ryan reined away and headed a couple of doors down to the hotel, tied the dun, and entered through the back door. Knowing Nico Vaca, Ryan figured he would be on the top floor, where the upper crust resided.

Quietly, he ascended the stairs until he reached the top floor and stood listening at the door into the hallway. He cracked it, then seeing no one in the hall, moved out.

Carefully, he moved down the hall, pausing and listening at each door, until he heard the sound of voices, loud, angry voices. He stilled, then reached for the door and slowly turned the knob.

At the same instant as he shoved the door open, a shot rang out. He snapped up his own weapon, but reeled back, thinking he'd been shot . . . as another man stumbled back into his arms. He caught the man, then seeing into the room, let him slowly slump to the floor.

Standing across the room, next to an open trunk, a smoking gun in her hand, was beautiful Felicia McCall, her long hair across her shoulders.

"What the hell?" Ryan managed.

He looked down to see the man on the floor was Nico Vaca, his eyes still open but blood bubbling from his nose, trickling from the side of his mouth, and staining his shirtfront from a hole in his chest. He was gasping like a baby bird at its mama.

"Vaca," Ryan said.

"Puta," was all the man managed, before his eyes glazed over.

"Felicia," Ryan said again, then realized the gun was now pointed at the middle of his chest. Carefully, he reholstered his weapon.

"What the hell?" he said again.

"He . . . he tried to rape me," she said, but she stood in her nightgown, and it wasn't torn, nor was the room out of order.

"I'm sorry," Ryan managed, although not believing what she'd declared. The way he'd heard it, she'd been with the man the better part of two years.

Ryan spun as someone topped the main stairs. A diminutive man who Ryan presumed was the night clerk.

Ryan rested his hand on the butt of his revolver and eyed the little man as he rounded the head of the main stairway. The man stopped short when he saw the upper torso of Nico Vaca on his back in the hallway.

"We have this under control," Ryan said to the man.

"I can see that," the man replied, his eyes wide, his face pale.

"Then go back to your desk," Ryan snapped, and the clerk turned and ran.

Ryan walked casually into the room, Felicia still standing stock still, the pistol still leveled on Ryan.

"I had to see you," Ryan said, ignoring the weapon.

"I'm glad you stopped by, Ryan," she answered, moving in front of the trunk so he could not see into it, where the box full of gold coins lay open. "I wanted to come see you in jail, but Nico wouldn't allow it."

"He won't mind now."

She ignored his sarcasm, but said nothing.

So Ryan offered, "I'm leaving, for parts north."

She smiled. "So am I, but east. There's nothing for me here."

"There was once."

"You . . . is that what you mean?"

Ryan shrugged so slightly it was barely noticeable. "I thought so. Maybe."

"Maybe," she said, "at one time. Not now."

"I guess feelings fade. You once said —"

"I've said a lot of things, Ryan. But yes, things fade away. And I'm going to fade away, back east somewhere."

"So . . . that's it?" Ryan asked.

"That's it. Hope things work out for you up north."

"And for you," Ryan said, backing toward the door.

"In another life," she said quietly, and he thought he saw a tear forming in her eye.

He paused at the doorway. "You're sure this isn't the right lifetime? It's the only one I'm damn sure of."

"Dead sure," she said, glancing down at Vaca.

Ryan could hear voices, then footfalls on the main stairway.

"Get out of here, Ryan," she said, wiping a tear away.

Ryan shrugged again, then strode toward the back stairway. In moments he was heading out of town at a canter. In an hour, he'd fallen in on the trail behind his kin.

The first time they stopped to wind the horses, Reese reined back beside him.

"You find that Vaca fella?"

"I did."

"He dead?"

"He is."

"You happy?"

Ryan gave him a sad smile. "As happy as I'm gonna be, at least in this lifetime."

"Then let's ride."

"Until we find a cantina. I owe the kin a drink of good Irish whiskey."

"You damn well do," Reese said, spinning his horse to keep up with the others, who were already raising dust in front of them.

"Hey, Reese," Ryan called out, and Reese looked back over his shoulder.

"How about lending me twenty bucks?"

Reese laughed, and yelled over the pounding of horses' hooves, "No problem, Ry, you're kin."